CW00507062

Beguiling the Earl

The Country House Romantic Mysteries
Book 2

by

Audrey Harrison

© Copyright 2023 by Audrey Harrison
Text by Audrey Harrison
Cover by Kim Killion

Dragonblade Publishing, Inc. is an imprint of Kathryn Le Veque Novels, Inc.
P.O. Box 23
Moreno Valley, CA 92556
ceo@dragonbladepublishing.com

Produced in the United States of America

First Edition September 2023
Print Edition

Reproduction of any kind except where it pertains to short quotes in relation to advertising or promotion is strictly prohibited.

All Rights Reserved.

The characters and events portrayed in this book are fictitious. Any similarity to real persons, living or dead, is purely coincidental and not intended by the author.

Find more about the author and contact details at the end of this book and the chance to obtain a free copy of The Unwilling Earl.

ARE YOU SIGNED UP FOR DRAGONBLADE'S BLOG?

You'll get the latest news and information on exclusive giveaways, exclusive excerpts, coming releases, sales, free books, cover reveals and more.

Check out our complete list of authors, too!

No spam, no junk. That's a promise!

Sign Up Here

www.dragonbladepublishing.com

Dearest Reader;

Thank you for your support of a small press. At Dragonblade Publishing, we strive to bring you the highest quality Historical Romance from some of the best authors in the business. Without your support, there is no 'us', so we sincerely hope you adore these stories and find some new favorite authors along the way.

Happy Reading!

CEO, Dragonblade Publishing

Additional Dragonblade books by Author Audrey Harrison

The Country House Romantic Mysteries
Persuading the Earl (Book 1)
Beguiling the Earl (Book 2)

Chapter One

London 1811

S AMUEL LANGFORD, EARL of Bentham, made his friends laugh as he rubbed his hand over his face in frustration. It was a rare display of emotion and only exhibited because he was in the company of his closest friends. "I swear, one way or another, my mother will be the death of me. Or better still, I might be forced to murder her," he groaned.

Mr. Dominic Leaver grinned at Samuel. "Is she insisting you marry in order to produce an heir?"

"That is the first reason she states, but soon goes on to the others. She insists I will only understand her motivation when I am in her position. She thinks constant nagging and pretending to ail will persuade me to find a wife and become closer to her by engaging in her questionable habits. In reality, it reminds me of why any woman I ever seriously consider marrying should be running for the hills at the prospect of a proposal from me. If I marry, Mother will have another individual to make life hell for," Samuel responded seriously.

"And that's before the poor woman has to put up with your shortcomings," Dominic said with a laugh.

"Dominic! That is unfair!" Patricia scolded her elder brother, but there was a laugh in her voice. She enjoyed the banter between them. Samuel and Dominic treated her as an equal in their conversations, being as quick-witted and intelligent as either of them. Her characteristics were often overlooked by men who chose to focus on the more eligible meek women in society, but she received respect and affection from her brother and his best friend.

She was tall and slender, with dark hair and eyes, not one of the fashionable petite blondes who vied to become the season's latest incomparable, especially as, at four and twenty, she was close to being considered an old maid. Brother and sister were very alike in colouring and height, but whereas it was seen as an advantage in Dominic, many thought it off-putting in Patricia.

It did not matter what anyone thought about her. There was only one man who had ever made her heart race and he was sitting opposite her. That he saw her as nothing but a friend had made her accept the fact that she would have to remain a spinster, thankful she had his friendship, if she could not have more.

"Probably true, though," Samuel acknowledged with a fond smile at Patricia—something that always brightened her day. "I keep trying to persuade her to remain in the country, but Mother insists there is a better chance of my marrying if she remains in town with me, although I know full well it is to stay close to the men she constantly seeks out. She refuses to listen when I try to explain that I have absolutely no intention of being leg-shackled anytime soon, and she must think I am a fool if I cannot see beyond her protestations of being here for my benefit."

"You are a popular dance partner; there must be ladies willing to consider you as a husband," Patricia reasoned, knowing full well some of the mutterings that followed Samuel whenever he appeared in society. He was not one of the most sought-after bachelors of the *ton*. Many people said he had a dangerous air about him, plus there were suggestions that he was not legitimate, which led some of them, but not all, to keep their distance. She hated that they did not see what she did, but then again, she felt privileged that she was one of the few to know the real Samuel.

"As you are well aware, dancing is a far cry from being wed, or some of the slow tops you have danced with would have stood a chance with you," Samuel pointed out, amused at the immediate reaction to his words.

Patricia grimaced. As always, Samuel was proving that he knew her almost as much, if not better, than her brother. It was a bittersweet thought. "I wish I could have refused half the dances I've been forced to endure, usually because Grandmamma has browbeaten some poor sap into asking for a dance. It is mortifying to be taller than your partner. I can feel their eagerness to get away from me the moment the music stops. On more than one occasion, I have been almost dragged off the dance floor in their hurry to return me to Grand-mamma."

"I am certain I have stirred more need to escape in the breasts of many young ladies," Samuel said, looking unperturbed at the thought.

"They are fools to believe malicious gossip, but you have not helped matters by creating such a rakish reputation." She might be overly fond of him, but she was not averse to telling him off when she felt it was needed.

"But is it gossip?" Samuel asked with a raised eyebrow.

"You are the image of your late father," Patricia stated. "It is no reflection on you that the tattlemongers suggest you are not his son. It doesn't matter anyway—your father doted on you. A pity you have not become more respectable; you play into the stories of being a libertine and rake by spending so much of your time in gaming hells and bawdy houses. Those are not the places to meet potential wives."

"Patricia!" It was Dominic's turn to berate his sister.

"What?" Patricia asked, completely unrepentant. "Am I to pretend such places do not exist? Are your sensibilities so easily shocked, brother?"

"It's not good *ton* to mention them in company," Dominic said mulishly.

"You and Samuel are hardly company," Patricia scoffed. "Anyway, to return to the point. Samuel needs to cultivate a more respectable reputation instead of the devil-may-care attitude he brings to most of the parties and balls he attends."

"It is more fun that way," Samuel said, his grin replacing normally serious features. "I like the title of Bawdyhouse Bentham."

Patricia tsked. "That's a name I would expect a schoolboy to have, not a mature man!"

Samuel looked at Dominic soberly. "Mature? Does your sister know me at all?"

"I think she is referring to the fact that you are approaching your dotage," Dominic responded.

Patricia threw a conveniently placed cushion through the air towards Dominic, which missed its mark, due to the fast movement of its target.

Dominic laughed at the reaction. "Touched a nerve have I?"

"You are both ridiculous," Patricia admonished. "Your mother is right in one respect, Samuel. You should be looking to marry. You aren't getting any younger, though not quite in your dotage as my brother suggests. Still, you do need an heir. Everyone with a family name to continue has that responsibility."

"Good God! This gets even more damning! I am only nine and twenty for goodness sake," Samuel groaned. "Not all of us have our lives planned out as you do, Patricia," he said. There was a hint of mockery in his tone, unusual for him when speaking to her.

Patricia refused to react to the barb—they were words which had been said many times before. "I have embraced the fact that I shall not marry, and you should try and accept your own future. When a decision is made about your lifestyle, it is quite freeing. If you accept the need to seek a suitable wife, you might find that you embrace the opportunity. It will certainly make your life easier, and your mother would have one less subject to lecture you on, which can only be a good thing."

Her tone was light, but it grieved her to think that one day he would not be in her company as much. They would probably not have the same easy banter with a wife added to the mix. It was a sad thought, but there was nothing she could do about it. If he had wanted her as his wife, something would have happened between them already.

"As much as it grieves me to disobey my mother, I cannot, in this instance, give in to her wishes. And you are still young, not in your dotage as you consider me, so there is still time for you to marry," Samuel pointed out. "Why on earth would you be so set on not finding a partner?"

"As my height is working against me, I am only reasonably handsome at best and have what can only be considered a moderate dowry, I have had to be realistic about my options."

"We aren't paupers!" Dominic responded hotly, never comfortable with being reminded they were one of the families whose riches had dwindled due to past relatives not being as fastidious with their fortune as future generations thought they should have been.

"I never said we were," Patricia said. "Do not think for a moment that I repine over anything in my life. I have you two, my own friends and Grandmamma. I need nothing else. I cannot see what a husband would add to my life."

"It is a practical way of looking at things, if what you said was true," Samuel acknowledged. "Still, it sounds an excessively dire way to exist, especially if your only option is to rely on Dominic and me for entertainment and good company. You have more spirit than most, Patricia. I cannot imagine you settling for the life of a spinster. You have fire in your blood and a sense of adventure. And don't all young women long for a love match?"

His words warmed her insides. He was always quick to complement her. It was a blasted shame he only saw her as a friend. "Maybe so, but I have yet to meet anyone who would not bore me to death, even if he could overlook my shortcomings. As I have said, I am content with my situation. Now all we have to do is find someone who is suitable for you."

"This is why my mother likes you so much," Samuel said with a grimace. "I think you must have spent too much time with her over the years. You clearly have similar views."

"I do not wish to cause offence, but I think not," Patricia said primly. "We have completely opposite opinions on how family life should be conducted."

Samuel smiled grimly, fixing his already neat cuffs. "What? You do not wish to flaunt your affairs under your husband's and your son's nose? If that is not the case, then you are indeed different from my mother, for she was an expert at it and still is."

"If I were to marry, I would never have affairs in the first place. Look what an impact such behaviour has had on your life. You do not deserve the censure you have received. And none of it because of your actions. Well, at least not in the early days, anyway." Patricia had to acknowledge that Samuel's reputation as a rake and a devil was of his own doing, but even before then, people were quick to make comments about the son being like his mother in order to keep the gossip mill running.

She had not endeared herself to many in the *ton* by constantly championing him whenever she heard derogatory comments aimed his way.

Patricia knew that Samuel would normally flare up at anyone speaking so plainly, but he was deeply attached to Dominic and Patricia which enabled them to get away with more. Dominic had been a steadfast friend since they were boys. Patricia had followed them whenever she could, and instead of despising her for the intrusion, they accepted her into their group, and the two easily became a three. She could see that hearing her words and the sincerity with how she delivered them had stirred emotion in Samuel. She felt bad that he always seemed to put himself down just as much as society did. She could tell that he was not sure how to react to her candour and the compassion in her eyes.

"I admire your sentiments, Patricia," he said quietly. "Anyone who remains faithful to their vows and considers that a vital part of a union will always be respected by me."

"That is reassuring to know," Patricia said glad that he had responded honestly, rather than flippantly. "Now all we have to do is find you a suitable wife who would also be sincere towards you."

"I do not think I should be concerned with my future wife's commitment to forsake any other. I think the problem lies with me," Samuel admitted.

"What do you mean?" Patricia asked.

Samuel shrugged. "I cannot promise anyone I would not stray from the marital bed. What if I turn out just like my mother?"

"Of course you will not! It is a real pity that you think in such a way—it shows little faith in your own feelings. I am sure you would never inflict the pain that you watched your poor father suffer as a result of your mother's actions." Once again, she was saying too much, but if she did not challenge him, no one would.

"I have yet to meet a woman where I have felt strong enough emotions that I would be sure we would be happy for the rest of our days. I do not think I am made for a happy marriage. I would not know what to do if I had the opportunity of embarking on one," Samuel acknowledged with a nonchalant shrug.

Patricia knew why he was professing the nonsensical words he had uttered. If he continued to play the uncaring aristocrat, he could not be hurt by anyone, for he certainly had suffered and had hated the way his father had struggled with his mother's infidelity.

"Well, in that case, Dominic and I will find you a match who will make you forget any other women exist, and you will settle happily into marital bliss."

"I want no part in schemes that are doomed to failure!" Dominic said with a barked laugh.

Samuel smiled at his friend before turning back to Patricia. "If you can find such a woman, I promise to marry her, but I promise you that there is no woman out there for me. She would have to have the patience of a saint to put up with me."

"True." Patricia smiled. "Still, I am determined to see you happy and if that means finding the perfect woman for you, then it is a task I willingly undertake, my best of friends."

"You will regret this, Samuel. You know you are going to regret it, don't you?" Dominic said, noticing the glint in Patricia's eyes.

"I am confident I will still be single in two years' time," Samuel responded easily. "There is not a woman alive who could make me even consider trusting her enough to marry her. For you know I could not stand by as my father did. Patricia, if you manage to find a chit who is foolish enough to become besotted with me, I promise to buy you the largest diamond necklace you can wear and marry the girl you have found without a single complaint."

Patricia smiled. "I shall start having a necklace designed so it is ready to wear at your wedding." She had a need to see him happy, which had urged her on. Though his happiness would be at the expense of hers, she was willing to make that sacrifice for him. She'd had a good childhood, but his had been horrendous. She needed him to have a happy future.

He was funny and relaxed in her company, but she had seen him in society enough to know that the act he put on in front of others was not the real Samuel. There had to be a way of helping him, whether he liked it or not. She could not bear the thought of him being lonely for the rest of his days. It would not be fair. After his upbringing, he deserved to experience love and affection by someone who he regarded in equal measure.

"I like your ambition, but in this regard it is misplaced." Samuel smiled at her.

"I pride myself on being one of the few people who know you, faults and foibles included, and it puts me in the perfect situation for choosing someone who will turn your head once and for all."

Dominic snorted. "Not even his pieces of muslin have lasted beyond a few months."

Samuel glared at his friend, clearly uncomfortable that those particular parts of his private life were being mentioned, "I would rather not have such topics spoken about in front of Patricia. She might not be a miss just out of the schoolroom, but I respect her too much to discuss such base topics. You curse your sister for knowing about gaming hells, yet here you are talking about mistresses. For goodness sake, mind your tongue!"

"She claims to know you. She needs to know this side of you too." Dominic shrugged with a grin caused by poking his friend enough to react. It was a silent challenge they always embarked on.

Patricia tsked. "I already know there is a line of broken-hearted widows who might not pester him anymore, but their sad eyes follow him around any ballroom he attends. It is pitiful to observe."

Samuel shifted in his seat. "You do exaggerate. They do nothing of the sort. And even if they do, you should not be noticing such things."

Laughing and shaking her head at him, Patricia wagged her finger. "I have to do something to entertain myself when sitting on the wallflower benches. It is quite amusing that one after the other has clearly thought she would be the one for you, but soon finds herself alongside the long line of previous conquests. It has kept my friends and me entertained for many an hour."

"Good God! I am the talk of the wallflower benches? I am never attending another ball," Samuel ground out, clearly uncomfortable that his actions were being observed by Patricia and her group of friends.

"That would be a pity, for I am determined to enjoy watching you, my good friend, falling head over heels in love. For I know that with the right woman, you would succumb."

Samuel snorted but it was Dominic who spoke. "My friend, you have my deepest sympathy because we are both fully aware of how determined Patricia is."

Patricia smiled at Samuel in that teasing way of hers, eyes sparkling with laughter. "You are concerned, aren't you?"

"Absolutely terrified," Samuel groaned.

Dominic barked out a laugh. "You are doomed!"

"I have a feeling you might be right."

Chapter Two

TRAVELLING IN HIS carriage to the place very few members of the *ton* would frequent unless they had no other choice, Samuel reflected on the morning spent with the Leavers. Smiling at Patricia's confidence, he shook his head. She was a minx, and he knew she would be outrageous in the type of women she would try to introduce him to over the coming weeks. He would look forward to rebuffing her at every point, for as highly as he thought of her, he would not be forced into a marriage—not even for Patricia.

He always felt lighter when he had spent the morning with them, or, should he say, *her*. Dominic was a good friend, and they did enjoy themselves, but Patricia had the ability to pull him out of the doldrums and make him laugh as no one else could. She was right when she stated that she knew him the best. Even Dominic did not pick up on the times when he felt particularly lost, but Patricia did. She rarely uttered a word about it, but her actions, the way she would touch his arm or speak to him, making him laugh, assured him that she was there and understood. He was lucky to have her in his life.

Becoming serious, he looked blindly out of the window as the houses and businesses passed. He was closer to Dominic and Patricia than to anyone else, but there was still a part of his life that he kept separate from them. He had been recruited some time ago by another member of the aristocracy who was looking for someone who did not mind revealing the individuals of society prone to thinking they were above the law.

At first, he had been surprised that he had been approached, but then had been told that his position on the edges of society gave him an advantage—he could watch and listen in private circles, which was a vital part of the role. He had been dismissive of the request at first but then the devil in him took over and he accepted. It was probably his desire for revenge on the same people who had whispered about his birthright and his respectability that drove him. After all, he was now effectively spying on them. He would never pass on false information, but he had no qualms about giving information on those involved in wrongdoing.

There was a reason he had not told his friends though; Patricia would know immediately why he had accepted the role and he could not stand to see the condemnation or disappointment in her eyes. Those had been his first thoughts, when in reality he could have told her. Yes, she would be disappointed but for some reason, he hated the thought that she did not know about that side of his life. If anything happened to him whilst on duty, he would not be able to explain to her and that bothered him.

He was now three years in and had been quite successful in the cases he had been on. But he'd been warned that this next assignment would not be an easy one. Walking into the offices at number four Bow Street, he bypassed the crowd of people waiting to be dealt with by the magistrate. He did not attend the address regularly, but he was there often enough that the sights, sounds and smells no longer made his nostrils flare with disgust or cause him to wish to bathe the moment he left. The Runners were not from his class, but he had no doubt that there were others like him. Always wary of new friendships, he had never tried to cultivate anything other than polite disinterest with anyone else in the establishment. He was a lone worker, and he was happy with that.

"Come in, take a seat," James Read, the man in charge of the Runners and magistrate of Bow Street, said to Samuel. "How are you?"

"Well, thank you." He sat on the only chair in the cluttered office, crossing his legs at the ankle, looking for all intents and purposes as if this was part of his normal routine, that he was just paying a visit to another gentleman. He saw the look of amusement from James and guessed his Runners would not be allowed to lounge so nonchalantly before their leader.

"I have a new case I hope you are willing to take on, though it is a little different from your usual ventures." James looked older than his years, his role never letting up, the chaos in his office testament to a man with too much to do and not enough time to do it.

"Oh?"

"There are thefts of high-value necklaces taking place among the *ton*, but in some instances, they are not being discovered immediately. The thief, or thieves, are expert at what they do. There are no signs of break-ins, but the jewels just disappear. It is obviously a well-planned operation and has been causing no end of problems."

"It isn't just an excuse made up by husbands who have had the jewels sold to finance their lifestyle?" Samuel asked.

"No, though we did think that initially," James answered with a rare smile. Being the head of Bow Street did not offer many opportunities for amusement. "It seems to be an inside job. The jewels are the only target."

"Servants?"

"Possibly, so that the thieves are able to gain access, but it is more likely they are not the ringleaders; they would not have the ability to get rid of such high-quality goods nor explain their sudden wealth. Some of the necklaces taken are worth more than most servants could earn in a lifetime."

"Then you think it is someone of consequence?"

"It is the only solution I can think of. But it is a devil of a situation, if it is."

"And because of that, you need someone on the inside, someone whose popularity will not be affected by the revelation that they have been spying on their own kind, if it should come to that," Samuel said with a faint smile.

"You are efficient and discreet. As well, you are readily admitted to all the ballrooms in London; that is my motivation in choosing you. It is not my intention to ruin your reputation."

"It is not good enough to destroy, but it is a stretch of the truth about my being welcome everywhere. Not every hostess is pleased to see me," Samuel said. "What is my role to be?"

"I want to partner you up with someone who will be wearing a necklace that will prove too tempting to resist."

"Someone? A partner? Certainly not. I work alone. You know full well I never want to have to consider another person—it can only cause complications."

"Unfortunately, we are in the position that unless we bring the thieves to us, we will constantly be arriving after the event."

"How are they getting rid of their loot? Surely there are avenues to explore there?"

"So far, very little has appeared in the stolen market. All our informants say there are no signs of the necklaces once their theft has been reported. Of course, this could mean they are getting rid of them before we are even aware of the theft, but our informants have been on the alert for some time now. The jewels could be broken down or sent abroad, but the fact is that because we are not able to find any sign of them, we need to change our current methods. We are getting nowhere with what we have tried so far, and believe me, I have been throwing resources at this for some time."

"Why is it so important? A bit of jewellery here and there is hardly something which threatens most of the population."

"I know. But we are looking at a lot of it—fifteen necklaces that we know about," James said. "What I tell you next is extremely confidential."

"As I speak to no one about my dealings with you, you have little to worry about on that score."

"I know and I trust you implicitly. But you should know that these thieves are getting more and more brazen. One particular necklace that was stolen belonged to Queen Charlotte."

"They got to her quarters?" Samuel was incredulous.

"No, she was on a visit to the Duke of Lancaster's London residence. It is very embarrassing for everyone involved. The duke, in particular, is keen to see the thieves caught."

"I see." Samuel was intrigued. How could something so valuable disappear without a trace?

"You see our dilemma. So we're trying a new approach. We would like you to work with a partner, someone who is trustworthy and discreet and who will not mind wearing the necklace we are using as bait."

"I can see the merit in your argument, but who do you have in mind? It would have to be someone with a strong nerve to put herself in the way of a thief."

"Ah, now hear me out before you snap my nose off," James said with a half-smile. "She will need a little coaching to get her up to snuff, but she has got potential and is no wilting flower. There have been no attacks on the women, but we have to be prepared for every eventuality, so I have chosen someone with that in mind."

Samuel groaned. "You do understand that my reputation will suffer even more if I start to escort an interloper around town, don't you? It will also not be very convincing that I would be putting myself out on behalf of someone else."

"We thought you could say she was some long-lost sister or cousin."

Glaring at James, Samuel had stiffened at the words. "And because my mother is a doxy, it is more likely to be believed?"

Having the decency to look abashed, James shrugged. "It was the best we could come up with."

"Damn you to the devil!"

James ignored the venom in Samuel's words and called for one of his officers to bring in Anne. The woman, for she must have been at least thirty, walked into the room, reasonably dressed, but the lines on her face and gaps in her yellowed teeth told of a harsh existence.

"Anne, meet Mr. Langford," James said, not mentioning the fact that Samuel was a member of the aristocracy.

"Pleased to meet you, darlin'," Anne responded in a broad London accent.

"And you," Samuel said, tone cold.

"I have told Anne something of the situation we are trying to stop, but the final decision is yours," James said.

"Aww, we'll get on fine, won't we, darlin'? A pity you'll be introducing me as your family. I said I would rather be engaged to ye, and now I've seen what a fine buck you are, I'm even more sorry. The fine wine and food will help ease my pain, though. Are we to visit more than one ballroom in a night? I am happy to have my fill in every place we go, for my legs don't dance as much as they used to."

"There is a lot more to discuss with Mr. Read," Samuel said coolly.

"Ah, I see how it is. Not good enough fer ye?" Anne asked, looking unperturbed that she was being so coldly rejected. "That's a pity, for I'm sure we would have found a way to rub along together." She winked at Samuel before turning to James. "I'll leave 'im with you, Mr. Read. 'E'll be an 'ard 'un to please, but I will 'appily oblige whatever you decide."

"Thank you, Anne. If we don't need your services, you will still be paid for your trouble," James said.

"You're a true gent, me darlin'," Anne said, moving to the door.

Samuel shook his head at James as Anne flounced out the door with one last leery look at him. "Really?" he asked incredulously.

"We do not have a lot of choice of women wishing to put themselves in danger. Fashionable ladies are more likely to need smelling salts if we were to even suggest doing such a thing," James defended himself. "At some point, there is a breach at the house being targeted. None of the ladies have known when their jewels were stolen, but all of the necklaces have disappeared from their chambers. Which means it is possible that the thief could be discovered in the process of carrying out the theft."

"That is a fair point. But I would be laughed out of every ballroom in the country if I accompanied the likes of her about town. And as for her staying with me, along with my mother, that is the stuff of nightmares," he finished with a shudder. "I refuse to even contemplate persuading my mother to believe my story, for after all, if she was to be my sister, my mother would surely remember giving birth to her? No, your plan is full of holes. You will have to think of an alternative."

"We need this case to be wrapped up. There are a lot of mutterings as to why we exist if we cannot protect the people at the top of society. Even the Regent is getting involved, saying that these brazen thefts are an attack on royalty. It is ridiculous, of course, but it gives him the opportunity to interfere into subjects which do not concern him. He would not have given a hoot about the thefts if his mother's necklace had not been stolen. I am constantly receiving orders to set my best men on the job, to send updates through, and the like. Yet again, there is no consideration for all the other work we do which directly or indirectly benefits the *ton*."

"That is a ridiculous accusation to be levelled at the organisation, especially when it could very well be someone in society committing the thefts."

"Exactly my thoughts, but you know full well what they are like. The reality of this situation is that it is not a case you can work alone. You need someone to help draw out the thieves; it is the only way we might discover who they are."

"I appreciate that, but I will choose who I work with, or I am not taking the case on," Samuel said.

James opened a drawer in his desk and took out a large cloth bag. "In that case, you might as well take this. It contains two necklaces. One is real, the other not. Make it known that the necklace was a present from the Queen; it will increase its desirability. The sooner you start, the better."

"Confident that I am going to find someone?" Samuel raised his eyebrows.

"I always have faith in you," James said.

"Then you are one of a very small group," Samuel said dryly. He accepted the bag, and without looking at it, he stood, pulling on his gloves and missing the somewhat satisfied smile on James's face—the smile of a man who believed that his plan to persuade Samuel to engage a partner had worked out perfectly.

"Choose carefully, for if it goes wrong…"

"I know. I will not be the only one affected," Samuel interrupted.

"I look forward to your updates." James stood and held his hand out, and after they shook, he nodded to Samuel. "Good luck."

"Luck has nothing to do with it; skill and ability are needed on every case."

He looked wryly at Samuel. "One day, you will be humbled by something. I hope I am around to see it."

Samuel laughed. "I doubt it," he said, leaving the office. Once outside, a frown replaced his lighter expression. It was going to be a devil of a job finding someone he was prepared to work with, someone who had the abilities and courage needed. Even the fact that the scheme was being driven by the Regent and the Queen might not be enough to persuade someone to help him.

For the first time in his life, Samuel felt hopeful that if he was able to solve this crime, the Regent might take notice of him. He wanted the case and was determined to solve it. Still, his standing in society was not the best because of his mother, and it would be nice for once if he was seen for the man he was, a decent person. If that made him shallow, then so be it. It would feel good to be on the right side for once.

"ABSOLUTELY NOT!"

"Oh, my goodness, yes!"

Not quite suppressing the smile Patricia and Dominic's outburst had caused, Samuel raised his hands in surrender. "It was a foolish thought. I should not have mentioned anything."

"No, you should not." Dominic glared at his friend.

Samuel groaned. "It is a devil of a thing, and I am coming to the conclusion that this will be the first case I will fail at."

"How long have you been working for Bow Street?" Dominic asked.

"A few years."

"And you never thought to mention anything?"

Samuel could see the disappointment on Dominic's face and was surprisingly affected by it. It was still a risk he had taken by revealing it, but he had come to the conclusion that it was the only thing he could do if he was to work with someone. "I did not wish for it to change things between us."

"How would it have done that?"

"Perhaps you would have worried about me more?" At the snort from Dominic, Samuel smiled. "It was just safer that way, for all of us. It would cause us all problems if I spoke about the cases I am working on."

"Why? I am discreet."

"But would you be able to act normally if you knew one of your friends was involved in underhanded practices? If you offered any hint that they were under suspicion, the game would be up and months of work could be wasted."

"But you could have been hurt or worse, and no one would have known," Patricia said, joining in with the reprimand.

"There are few who would care if I were to disappear."

"I hate it when you speak so dismissively about yourself!" Patricia scolded. "We care and value you. I wish you would believe it."

Samuel moved from his usual spot near the fireplace, took hold of Patricia's hand and kissed it. "I know you do, and trust me when I say that I treasure that fact. Ignore my flippancy."

"Then I would have to ignore more than half of what you say," Patricia replied, causing Samuel to laugh.

"Good point." He moved back to the fireplace, resting his arm on the mantelpiece, his usual frown back in place. "I am sorry. I should not have even considered you for a moment," he said to Patricia. "Dominic is correct; it is a stupid idea."

"I do not see why you should not have considered me," Patricia said with a huff. "I think it is the perfect solution to your quandary. You know I am not some flibbertigibbet, and I am calm in a crisis. As well, everyone knows we are friends, so there would be no speculation about us being together at a ball. I think it is one of your better ideas."

"I will not allow you to become embroiled in something which could put you in danger," Dominic said.

"Oh, you will not allow it, will you not?" Patricia asked archly. "And since when have you become my keeper?"

"As the head of the family, I do have some responsibility for you. And before you take me to task, yes, I know you are of age," Dominic responded.

"I think Grandmamma would have something to say on your claim," Patricia replied airily. Patricia and Dominic had lost their parents when they were young. Their grandmother, a force to be reckoned with, had brought them up when they'd been orphaned. The brother and sister adored their grandmother, but their shared loss had made them even closer than they were before.

"You know what I mean."

"This is a real adventure. And for once, I could feel that I was doing something useful. Knitting socks for the poor is not very exciting though I know it is vital work."

"It is also safer."

She turned to Samuel. "Would you do all that you could to protect me if there was a problem?"

"I would."

"Has there been any other instance when these thieves have hurt the women they have targeted?"

"No. The thefts have only been discovered some time later."

"And that is why I object," Dominic interrupted. "The stakes have changed. You are aiming to reveal the identity of the offender, so Patricia is more at risk than any of the others were."

"I promise to protect her as if she was my own," Samuel said, meaning every word, surprised at the force of protective feeling he felt toward her.

"The thief will only be tackled when I have been robbed; that part is not going to change. They do not take the jewellery from the person, so I will not be in any danger."

"But what if you are only with Grandmamma in the house when the thief strikes? What then?" Dominic asked his sister.

"If I can impose on your hospitality, I would remain in your home for the duration of the case, though we would obviously not be making that snippet of information widely known," Samuel said.

"What will your mother's opinion of leaving her to her own devices be?" Dominic asked.

"As she is currently feigning illness, which has been caused by her latest conquest finding a wife of his own who is younger and prettier than Mother, I doubt she will notice my absence. But I will tell her I am spending time with a friend."

"Which she will interpret to mean a mistress," Patricia supplied. For some reason, the thought disappointed her.

"Thankfully, in this case, that is indeed what she will presume, and though she will no doubt curse me to the devil for not meeting her demands about finding myself a wife, she will not comment on the fact that she thinks I have a lightskirt. It is one of the very few advantages of having a mother with a worse reputation than your own."

Patricia immediately felt for her friend. "I hate that she has caused you problems. It is not fair that people's conduct towards you is influenced by her actions."

"There is no need to worry about me." Samuel smiled at her. "I promise I am made of stern stuff."

"As am I," Patricia said, giving Dominic a pointed look. "How can I turn down a task which will cause me no hardship, when the poor Queen is involved. She deserves to have her jewels returned after what she has gone through with the King."

"It is not fair to use the royal aspect of this case," Dominic grumbled.

"But it is most important. And if Bow Street is coming under pressure to find the thief, surely it is our moral obligation to help."

"I hate that you have twisted this around, simply so you can justify your involvement. On your head be it," Dominic muttered.

"When do we start?" She rubbed her hands together. "Since Amelia married and all the excitement around her betrothal is over, life has been dull. This is just what I need."

"I find it disturbing that you consider your friend being compromised and her being held captive by a killer, entertainment," Dominic said, reminding his sister of the reality of the time she was considering an adventure.

"It all worked out well in the end," Patricia said. But her cheeks were tinged with a blush at Dominic's reprimand.

"Leave her be. We both understand exactly what she means," Samuel said, immediately defending Patricia. "I need to decide what ball would be a suitable start. I want it to be a large event, something big enough to tempt any thief. We will deck you out in jewels. I can then lay in wait for when they come to relieve you of your necklace."

"That sounds like a good idea. Why not use Amelia's ball as the event?" Patricia suggested. "They are planning a large party in a week; you must have had an invitation."

"I have. It is worth considering," Samuel said.

"I think it is a splendid idea," Patricia responded.

"You would," Dominic ground out.

"Oh, live a little," Patricia teased.

"I have a good mind to tell Grandmamma what you are intent upon."

"You wouldn't!" Patricia exclaimed.

"If I did, you would be sent off to the countryside for your own good."

"But being the best of brothers, you would never do that to me, would you?" With exaggerated pleading eyes, Patricia stared at her brother, making him smile despite his reluctance to agree to the scheme.

"Blast you, no, I will not. But it will be on your head when she finds out and roasts you for acting in such a foolish manner."

"She will be none the wiser."

"And that is the most idiotish thing you have ever uttered," Dominic said with all the derision only a loving brother could muster.

Chapter Three

"**I** AGREE WITH your brother. It is very risky," Amelia, wife of the Earl of Douglas and one of Patricia's best friends, said when Patricia had explained what they intended to do at the ball.

"Says the one who thought it was wise to search the bedchamber of a man whose morals were questionable, to say the least. A man who had been overheard threatening to compromise you," Patricia said of the situation in which Amelia had found herself not that long ago.

"I had an escort of sorts, and I have since admitted that it was fool-hardy, albeit after the event. It could have ruined me and resulted in me marrying a brute and a gambler, if it had not turned out so well with Richard," Amelia said, a smile on her lips.

Patricia could not spoil the dreamy look on her friend's face whenever she mentioned her husband. All Amelia's friends adored Richard for convincing Amelia that she was beautiful and worth loving when an accident had caused life-long injuries to her body, affecting her self-confidence. She was a pretty woman with rich auburn hair and eyes like silver, but her injuries had forced her withdrawal from society. And when she had returned, those same injuries had made her remain disinterested in obtaining a match, fearing a rejection in the marital bed.

"And I will be fine with Samuel."

"You know his reputation. Are people not going to talk when they see you together more than usual? I know you normally dance with him on the occasions he makes an appearance at an entertainment, but this is going to be wholly different," Amelia cautioned.

Before Patricia could respond, the door opened and Samuel walked in. His arrival was never announced by the staff as he was such a frequent visitor to the house. Patricia smiled and stood to greet him. His regular visits were often the highlight of her days.

"Good day, ladies. Jones said you were with Lady Douglas, and I did not think you would mind me joining you," he said as he bowed to them and kissed Patricia's hand, resplendent as usual in his fine wool frock coat, breeches and riding boots with a shine that Brummell would approve of. His attire was that of a nonesuch, perfect and expensive. Patricia took a moment to admire her friend. He was handsome, with jet hair and piercing blue eyes, eyes which she loved to watch change shade as his emotions played out.

"Of course not." Patricia smiled at him. "In fact, we were just talking about you."

"Oh?" Samuel was immediately on the alert, though he sat down at Patricia's request.

"I have taken Amelia into my confidence," Patricia said.

Samuel closed his eyes for a moment and gritted his teeth. "Why?" he ground out. "You pride yourself on not being a gossip, and I told you how important it was not to tell a soul."

Amelia looked at Patricia with an amused smile.

"I do not gossip," Patricia responded. She knew her tone was tart, but she could not help it. She was sure she looked somewhat shame-faced, as well. "I was confiding in my trusted friend and the person who is holding the ball where we hope to tempt the thief with my jewellery. I thought it necessary in case something happened whilst we were there."

"I mean no disrespect or affront when I object to you knowing our plans, Lady Douglas," Samuel said to Amelia. "It is just the more people who know, the less likely we shall have success with our task. There are now four of us, when there probably should only be two, though I take responsibility for telling Dominic." Still, he looked to be barely tamping down his frustration.

"None taken." Amelia smiled. "I will not utter a word to anyone, not even my husband, but there is one flaw in your plan."

"Amelia!" Patricia hissed, knowing what her friend was going to say and not wishing to see the disdain and dismissal on Samuel's face at what Amelia was going to utter.

"Oh?" Samuel asked, with a raise of his eyebrows at her forwardness.

"As I have pointed out to Patricia, it will appear odd if you are to spend more time together than you usually do."

"We see each other most days," Patricia said.

"Yes, but not in the ballrooms of society. Many people are not aware of the long-standing friendship that exists between your families," Amelia continued. "I think if you just go ahead with your scheme without some sort of explanation, it will draw the type of attention you would prefer to avoid."

Samuel did not respond but seemed to be mulling over Amelia's words. Patricia looked between them, hoping one of them would speak. She could sense that Samuel was likely to alter his plans, and she felt panic at the thought of no longer being involved. But at least he had not reacted as poorly as she had expected.

Eventually, she was forced to put her own view across before Samuel decided to end their charade before it even started. "I refuse to change plans now! You agreed I could help. You cannot change your mind at this stage. Amelia's ball is only days away," she said.

"There is no need to alter anything. There is a solution," Amelia said, mischief in her eyes.

"What is it?" Patricia asked eagerly, for once failing to notice that Samuel's posture had stiffened at Amelia's words.

"It might sound ridiculous, but it would make things so much easier for you both. You need to make an announcement of you being engaged!" Amelia said with glee.

Samuel sat forward in his seat and put his head in his hands. "This is exactly the reason why I work alone."

"Is a false engagement to me so repulsive?" Patricia asked. She tried to make her tone light, but his words and reaction had affected her more than she expected.

"It should be to you," Samuel said, knowing and hating that he had hurt Patricia unintentionally.

"Why? We would both know that it was not real," Patricia said. She cursed her instant reaction of pleasure at Amelia's suggestion. She would do to remember that even if Samuel agreed to it, it would be a farce and nothing more.

"But society would think that it is genuine, and your future prospects could be damaged as a result," Samuel said gently.

Patricia waved her hand in dismissal, recovering her usual zeal. "I do not give a fig what anyone thinks, and I am hardly fighting off suitors. It might help my reputation; I would be seen as the one to tame Bawdyhouse Bentham."

Amelia burst out laughing at Patricia's words, but Samuel shook his head at Patricia.

"You are incorrigible," he said.

"That is exactly why you wish to marry me." Patricia grinned. "But I should warn you that all too soon, I will call off the engagement and leave you broken-hearted."

"If you reject me, I will never recover," Samuel said, hand on his heart.

"Good. Then it is settled?"

"I must be out of my mind, but I suppose so," Samuel said. "Though Dominic will probably explode when we tell him. What are you going to tell your grandmother?"

"It would make it easier if she believed the engagement to be real. As you said, the fewer people who know the truth, the better. I do not see any harm in letting her know that there is someone out there who is willing to put up with me."

"You should not undervalue yourself; you are far preferable to most of the women of my acquaintance," Samuel responded.

"But not all?" Patricia said archly.

Laughing, Samuel seemed to try to scowl at her and failed. "It was a figure of speech. Of course, you are the one I regard the highest."

"Excellent, then we are engaged! Oh no!" Patricia suddenly exclaimed, looking mortified. "We cannot."

"Whyever not?" Amelia asked.

"The bet," Patricia said, looking at Samuel.

"This sounds even more interesting than trying to find a thief," Amelia said.

Samuel rolled his eyes. "She is determined to find me a wife."

"We have a wager, and I want that diamond necklace," Patricia huffed. "If we pretend we are to marry, then I cannot spend my time seeking out a wife for you."

"Good."

"There is a diamond necklace at stake? That is an extremely large wager," Amelia said in some surprise.

"I agreed to it because I knew she was never going to win," Samuel said with confidence.

"It would not surprise me if you had primed Amelia to suggest this scheme just to stop you from losing."

Samuel laughed. "I have not the imagination nor level of concern at your plans to think up such a thing."

"Amelia?" Patricia asked, eyes narrowed.

"I refuse to answer that on the grounds that it is a ludicrous suggestion."

"What do we do now?" Patricia asked. "I refuse to have such a disadvantage while there is a time limit on our wager."

Sighing, Samuel lifted his hands and rubbed them over his face. "Fine. The bet starts after we have finished with this."

"You give me your word?"

"Of course."

"Excellent! It seems the engagement is back on!"

"Thank goodness for that," Samuel said, surprising himself that he meant the words.

They looked at each other, both grinning, until Amelia coughed slightly. "In that case, the ball will announce the engagement to wider society, but make sure your family knows beforehand. I want no family dramatics at the ball—I have my own respectability to maintain. Once the announcement has been made, it will be a perfect opportunity for you to remain together but to go around accepting the congratulations from everyone."

"They will be commiserating with you," Samuel said.

"Then they do not know your true value," Patricia responded.

Samuel seemed struck by her words. His cheeks coloured a little as he looked at Patricia warmly. "You are the best of friends."

"She certainly is, and I expect you to look after her," Amelia said, standing while pulling on her gloves.

"Oh, there is no need to worry on that score. Dominic has threatened all sorts of violence if one hair of her head is harmed," Samuel said, also standing and bowing to Amelia.

"There will be a long line behind him," Amelia said. "Are you going to tell our other friends the truth?"

Patricia glanced at Samuel and nodded at his slight shake of the head. "No. I would like to, but I understand why I must not. I will not like lying, but I will keep up the deception when around them," she said of their three other friends who made up their small group. "When it is revealed, they will understand," Amelia said.

"At least Caroline is still on her travels," Patricia said. "I will just not mention anything in my letters."

"Isabelle and Sophia might."

"I will say I want to tell Caroline in person," Patricia said.

"It worries me slightly that you come up with solutions so easily. I think I have just tied myself to a managing woman," Samuel said, a smile playing on his lips.

"Who is a managing woman?" The voice of Mrs. Leaver, Patricia's grandmother, was heard at the doorway.

Samuel and Patricia glanced at each other. Then seeming to resign himself, Samuel shrugged, giving Patricia control of making the announcement to the person who had raised her since her parents had died.

"I, or should I say we, have news," Patricia started, making a quick decision and walking to Samuel, placing her hand in his, reassured when he squeezed it in support. "We have decided that we cannot live without each other and are to marry."

"You have done what?" Enid Leaver looked stunned.

"And this is the moment I should leave you," Amelia said.

"Coward," Enid growled at Amelia.

"Oh, most certainly." Amelia smiled at the older woman. "I have seen you in action before and have no intention of repeating the experience if I can avoid it."

Amelia's words brought a slight smile to Enid's lips, but it soon died when she turned back to Patricia and Samuel. "You had better start explaining yourselves and fast."

"YOU REALLY SHOULD not allow her to speak to you like that," Samuel said over an hour later when they had both been interrogated, and then abandoned, by Enid for a prior appointment. Neither had been so glad to see the back of someone in their lives. It had taken all of

Samuel's willpower not to shout at Enid at some of the things she had said—surprisingly not when her derision had been aimed at himself. But he had not liked the way she had spoken to Patricia.

"She is not usually like that; she has always been my biggest supporter. I know her words come from a place of love. She was simply shocked that there had been no hint of a match between us. You know how her group likes to be at the forefront of the gossip," Patricia defended her relative.

"Does such an extreme reaction really come from a place of affection? You could say that of my mother, as well. I, on the other hand, choose to take the more realistic view that it is her own needs that drive her actions and demands. She even uses emotional blackmail with regards to her supposed illnesses, which appear and disappear as the mood takes her, or when a lover is being inattentive."

"I do not understand how Grandmamma would be acting selfishly," Patricia said, not disagreeing with his assessment of his mother. Having spent time in her company over the years, Samuel was not being harsh, just realistic.

"You are a single woman, who had accepted spinsterhood, though as mentioned previously, that was a ridiculous presumption at four and twenty. But one thing your decision did was give Mrs. Leaver a companion for as long as she needs one. Someone who would be beside her for the rest of her days."

Patricia looked to deny the accusation but then shrugged. "It would be understandable for her to make that assumption. I know she would support me if she thought I had secured a happy future."

"Though she did not seem very happy when you announced our engagement, which puts a severe dent in your argument."

"It was the shock. Once the news sinks in, she will be fine."

"I never saw her so overwhelmed when you announced it."

Laughing, Patricia patted his arm. "That is because she knows the reputation of the rake I am to marry."

Narrowing his eyes, Samuel leaned close to her. "Are you up to the task of taming the rake?"

Feeling a little breathless at the change in Samuel's tone, she could not avoid glancing at his lips. They curved up slightly in the smile he had when he was trying not to show his amusement. She had never noticed before quite how appealing that smile was, or how the levity he was feeling made his blue eyes take on a deeper hue.

Gathering her wits and forcing herself to act normally, she punched him lightly in the shoulder. "Stop funning with me. We both know you are completely feral. No one could tame you."

"Wild for you, my sweet, just for you," Samuel responded, grabbing her hand and kissing her palm for longer than he should. Then swiftly standing, he bowed to her and bid her good day.

Patricia was standing near a chair, and she considered it a good thing as she sank into it. She had always been fond of him—perhaps a little too fond if she was being totally honest with herself—but when he had spoken to her in such a way, it was as if her world had shifted slightly. She had suddenly understood why the widows he had discarded followed him with sad eyes, for his intensity made one hot in a way which was most disconcerting but not unpleasant. In fact, she hoped most fervently that it was an experience she would have many times during their false engagement, for the warmth which had rushed through her body as a response to his breath tickling her cheek had sent tingles where she had never felt them before.

"It is not real," she muttered, trying to calm herself down. "He is playing a role, and so are you, and you had better not forget that or you will spoil everything." Her words were stern, and she nodded after uttering them, as if she trying to convince herself. But then she undermined her words by flopping against her seat, hands over her face, and groaned.

Chapter Four

H E WAS A blasted fool, Samuel thought as his carriage trundled slowly through the streets of London. What the devil had he been thinking of? If Dominic had even a hint of how he had just behaved, he would call him out, and rightly so. Rubbing his hand over his face, not caring whether his hair stuck up as he tugged on it in frustration, he grumbled to himself. He should have never asked for her help. It was his own damn fault that he had not thought it through properly. And already they were in too deep to turn away from the farcical situation.

Blast it, he should have refused the case once he learned there was a need for him to work with another. He was not good with others, never had been and was not about to change for anyone. He could excuse the fact that he had thought that Patricia was the only one he would trust enough to help him. A mistress would have likely relished playing the part, but her feelings would likely get in the way. Patricia had never had an agenda, as so many of his mistresses had. They often thought they would eventually persuade him into matrimony, though he told them from the start that he was looking for a diversion and nothing more.

Patricia had been steadfast throughout his life as his supporter and advocate, though that job was certainly not an easy one. She was adventurous, too, wanting to sail, swim and shoot just as they had done when they were children. Full of pluck and a good friend to have.

Then why the deuce had he just acted like the rake he was towards the woman he thought the most of?

He had *flirted* with Patricia! The sister of his best friend. Pausing, he shook his head. No. She was as much his friend as Dominic was. He valued her more highly than any other woman of his acquaintance, though he had suggested otherwise. So why the devil was he risking their friendship by toying with her?

Looking blindly out of the carriage window, he thought back to Patricia's response. Her chocolate-coloured eyes had widened in surprise when he had kissed the palm of her hand, but she had not pulled away. She should have scolded him as she had done when he had teased her about taming him, yet she had barely uttered a goodbye when he had departed. Why had she not cursed him and thrown him out of at least the room, if not the house, at his foolish actions?

More importantly, why did he feel a frisson of excitement at the fact that she had unconsciously leaned towards him? No. Thoughts like that had to stop. She was a green girl, and he would not repay the good deed she was doing him by making her into some sort of prize to win. She deserved so much more than he could ever offer. His thoughts were foolish in the extreme. He had never before considered her anything more than a friend, but then, they talked about a fake engagement and everything changed? He was acting like a mooncalf, idiot that he was.

The last thought he had before his carriage came to a stop at his house was that one day she would meet someone for whom she would cast aside her nonsensical ideas of remaining a spinster. Whoever was fortunate enough to win Patricia would be one lucky devil indeed. And for the first time in his life, he experienced a pang of jealousy.

"ENGAGED? TO LORD Bentham?" Isabelle asked her friend, not attempting to hide her incredulity.

"This is not a good start!" Patricia laughed but glanced in appeal to Amelia, who was there to support her. "Are you so surprised that he could fall in love with me?"

"Not at all!" Isabelle exclaimed. She was usually quiet and reserved, often seeming on the fringes of their group when next to her more confident friends. "It is just the reputation he has."

"But Patricia has known him for years," Amelia said.

"And he is nothing like the man you see in a ballroom."

"He has an impressive glower," Sophia said.

"He has never glowered at me," Patricia said. Her words made her pause. It was true, she had never been the victim of one of Samuel's well-known scowls. In fact, he always seemed to laugh when in her company. It was an awareness of his conduct when in her presence that warmed her and made her wonder, but she pushed that thought aside. She was being silly. One did not treat friends the same way you treated those who had been derogatory and gossiped about you.

"I would hope he has not," Sophia said.

"Our ball is the perfect opportunity to announce it to the world, especially as it will take the attention away from us," Amelia said.

"You should have all the attention. It is your first large party since you were wed," Patricia said. "We could announce it earlier. I am sorry, I had not considered that we would be taking the limelight away from Richard and yourself."

"We would have had other parties, but for the fact that we had an obsessed former love and her murdering husband to contend with first," Amelia said. She was making light of what had been a difficult and dangerous time. "Both Richard and I welcome that there is some good news to announce on the evening. Neither of us wishes to be the focus of attention any more than we need to be."

"In that case, it sounds like perfect timing," Isabelle said. "Congratulations, Patricia. Forgive my outburst. Lord Bentham is very fortunate to have secured you, especially as you were so intent on rejecting anyone who asked."

"I did, but then I realised Samuel meant more to me than anyone I had met." Patricia felt discomfort at deceiving her friends, but she had given her word to Samuel, and she would not let him down. She noticed the look Amelia had shot in her direction as she had spoken, and her cheeks reddened at how sincere her words were.

"When are you to marry?" Sophia asked.

"I have no idea!" Patricia laughed, but it felt strained to her own ears. "We have not made our engagement public. We'll let the news sink in first, and then we will decide what we wish to do next."

"Have you told the Dowager Countess?" Sophia asked.

"Yes. Let me just say that her raptures could be heard all over the house," Patricia said with a grimace. "She has said that once I am married, it will give me a freedom that I would not otherwise enjoy. She welcomed me to the family and then said that she would advise me on being discreet. She is a strange creature. Afterward, she turned to Samuel and said she knew he would not be like his father, for he was already a man without morals! For a moment, I thought Samuel was going to strangle her, but I managed to get him out of the room before he did or said something he would regret."

"I suppose you have the advantage over others in that you know her a little. Imagine what a stranger would have thought at hearing those words," Sophia said.

"Indeed. Still, I found them shocking, and I have never seen Samuel so annoyed," Patricia replied honestly. "I felt so sorry for him. I could not believe that she was telling the woman he was marrying that it was acceptable for them both to have affairs. Who would do that to their own son?"

"Who would think it acceptable to say to anyone, relation or not?" Sophia chipped in.

"That woman is unbelievable," Isabelle said. "The poor man. How could she be encouraging you to have affairs before you are even wed!"

"I have promised Samuel that I would never do such a thing," Patricia said with sincerity. She felt a little out of sorts but tried to hide it. She had not expected to need to reveal so much to make the situation convincing. What had felt like a jest when it was first mentioned was beginning to feel more discomforting the deeper the story had to develop. It was partly that she was deceiving her friends, and though it was for valid reasons, it did not rest easy. But more troublesome was the more she spoke about Samuel and the engagement, the more she began to wish it were true herself.

"Let us talk about the ball," Amelia interjected, lightening the mood.

PATRICIA ENTERED THE ballroom, heart pounding, with a fluttering in her stomach. Her hand rested on Samuel's arm, and she smiled up at him when he reached out with his free hand and squeezed hers in response to her unconscious iron grip.

"It will be fine, do not worry. I will protect you. But I am not expecting anything to happen tonight," Samuel said, looking down at her with a wink.

"I am not sure which thought worries me the most, making the announcement of our engagement or looking at everyone and considering whether or not they are a thief."

Samuel raised an eyebrow at her. "I could be offended at that."

"But you aren't." Patricia grinned at him. "And that is the reason we make the perfect pair. I do not need to try and pretend I am some meek and feeble miss, and you can complain and growl as much as you like, and I will not think any worse of you."

"Complain and growl? Good grief! Is that what you think I do?"

"Not at all. As I told my friends when they were aghast at our engagement, you never glower at me." She was teasing him and thoroughly enjoying herself, relaxing once more.

"You little minx," he muttered. "I will be glowering at you if you continue with your impertinence."

"It is worth noting that when you do marry for real, you will require a poor sap of a girl who will be so afraid of you that she will never utter a word, allowing you to forget she is even there! I need to keep that in mind, as I also spend my time considering who you would suit."

Samuel laughed, causing a few curious looks to be aimed in their direction. "And it will be a brave man who takes you on," he replied.

Patricia swallowed. His words had been said with no hint of malice, in the same way she was teasing him, but to her surprise, they had stung a little, more than a little if she was being honest. "There is not a man I would consider marrying, so it is a moot point," she said stiffly.

Samuel shot her a look, but thankfully her grandmother chose that moment to approach them.

"You are determined to go through with this, then," she said, sounding unconvinced. She looked pointedly at the necklace Patricia was wearing, having been told it was an engagement gift from Samuel—one of the family's treasures, given to his grandmother by the Queen many years prior. "A least you don't scrimp on your baubles; that is to your credit."

"Grandmamma! It is hardly a bauble! It belonged to the Queen!" Patricia exclaimed, her hand touching the necklace. It looked magnificent—deep red rubies surrounded by tiny diamonds, making each cluster appear as delicate flowers. When she had first seen it, she needed some convincing that it was a good idea for her to wear it.

"This is a more expensive necklace than I have ever worn," she had said, holding it in her hands, feeling the weight of it.

"Do not worry, the one that will be locked away in your jewellery box is made of paste," Samuel had explained as he had fastened it around her neck. It had been an intimate gesture, causing goosebumps to ignite across her body, but the presence of Dominic had stopped her mind from running away with itself too much, though she had struggled to suppress a shiver of pleasure when Samuel's fingertips had touched her neck.

Now she was feeling protective of the jewels, as if they had been truly given as a token of affection. And they were indeed very valuable, which was good. Her grandmother, astute woman that she was, could sniff out a falsehood far too easily. "It is a beautiful gift for which I am truly thankful."

"Aye, well, do not let this be a one-time occurrence," Enid said to Samuel. "I know it is too easy to take a wife for granted, especially someone like Patricia."

"Why especially like Patricia?" Samuel asked.

Patricia noticed the stiffening of his body as they stood side by side and felt oddly pleased that he was annoyed on her behalf.

"You think you have secured someone who will be grateful to you for choosing her," Enid said.

"I think you will find it is the other way around," Samuel replied.

Enid snorted. "She might be a green girl, but I am not. Earl or not, I will be watching you. She is precious to me."

"And to me," Samuel said. He steered Patricia away from her relation and headed towards Richard and Amelia, who had greeted their guests and had now joined the crowded ballroom. "When we marry, we will be taking an extremely long wedding trip away from your grandmother," Samuel said as they made their way through the throng.

Patricia laughed. "Fine, you demanding brute." She was fully aware that it was best to stay in character now they were surrounded by people, but it did create an unexpected pang of longing to shoot through her at his words.

Amelia and Richard greeted them warmly. "Are you ready for this?" Amelia asked her friend.

Patricia nodded. "Yes."

Richard stopped the music while he made the announcement. There were cheers and applause, but the reaction fooled neither Patricia nor Samuel. She was only known well by a few in society, being a spinster with little dowry meant that a woman was barely noticed by the people at the top of the tree.

Samuel, on the other hand, was an earl with a fortune. Though he was considered irascible and disparaging, many of the single women and their mothers suffered a moment of disappointment at Richard's words. A title and a healthy, well-run estate were not so easily dismissed, whatever the character and background of the earl. If his legitimacy was in question, he had been accepted by the old earl and had inherited without challenge, so that fact could be overlooked by most wishing to make a good match and who had not been able to attract more amenable partners. Many people came to offer their congratulations, mostly so they could inspect, close up, the woman who had secured the aloof earl.

After twenty minutes, Samuel noticed the strained look on Patricia's face. "Come, let us retire to the refreshment room. I can see you have had enough."

Patricia shot him a grateful look and, putting her hand on his arm, allowed herself to be led into the smaller anteroom off the ballroom.

Letting out a breath of relief when Samuel handed her a glass of champagne, she took a refreshing gulp. "There is a lot to be said for being on the edge of society. How on earth do you put up with that false sincerity all the time?" she asked.

Samuel smiled. "I do not usually. You know full well what my reputation is and the rumours which surround me. I do not entertain the few people unwise enough to try and get close. I prefer it that way.

This is a strange situation for us both, but a perfect opportunity for the thief to have a good look at your necklace."

"Does it not unnerve you to think we might be being watched?"

"Not really," Samuel admitted. "Is it too much for you? We could leave now if you like. I would not wish to upset your equilibrium; you have already done so much by putting up with the inane platitudes of insincere people."

"You must really think me a poor creature." Patricia scowled at him. "I asked if it unnerved you. I did not express any distress of my own."

"No, you did not. I just presumed..."

"Well don't. There is nothing more annoying than being considered a weak and feeble specimen. I can assure you that although I do not have much experience, I am not one for hiding away from a task. I committed to this scheme, and I will see it through."

Samuel smiled at the tartness of her words. "I shall never make that error again."

"Good. Does this mean we have survived our first argument?" The twinkle in her eyes had returned.

"It would appear so."

They were interrupted by Dominic's approach. "You are to have some competition, Bentham," he said, picking up a glass of champagne and immediately emptying it.

"With regards to...?" Samuel asked.

"My sister. Grandmamma has discovered some long-lost cousin of ours and is very keen to introduce him to Patricia. I think, in her eyes, he is a more appealing suitor."

"But I am engaged!"

"Until you are actually wed, it seems your grandmother is determined to make you see sense, or at least show you some alternatives. I would be offended if this situation was otherwise, but I suppose I have nothing to complain about for now," Samuel responded dryly. He was maintaining his nonchalant air, but it obviously stung that Enid seemed determined to separate them.

"It is strange, for she has always welcomed you into the house," Dominic mused.

"That was before I decided to whisk Patricia away from under her nose. A friend can be tolerated in areas that a relative cannot," Samuel said.

"It seems a bit hypocritical to me," Dominic said. "You aren't a bad 'un, no more than any other single man at any rate."

"Thank you, I think," Samuel said dryly. "Perhaps she has heard a little more of my exploits because of our friendship."

"Possibly, but everyone knows that an unmarried man behaves a lot differently than a married one."

"Most of the time, there are others…" Samuel started.

"I suppose so, but I would have thought she would have a higher opinion of you."

"Never mind what she thinks of Samuel. How could she think I would be so fickle?" Patricia asked in disbelief. "This is not like her. She has been acting strangely since we told her about the engagement."

"She is probably up to something, I would not put anything past her," Dominic said.

Samuel could have cursed Enid to the devil, but when she approached their group not ten minutes later, he felt a stab of raging jealousy that he had never suffered before. Moving to Patricia's side, he made the unorthodox gesture of wrapping his arm around her waist and pulling her close.

Hearing her sharp intake of breath, he looked down to see a flush of surprise and confusion on her cheeks.

"I refuse to give you up to anyone, no matter how handsome he is," he said quietly, his words as much a surprise to him as they seemed to Patricia if the look she shot him was anything to go by.

The stranger was indeed handsome, with blond hair and green

eyes, and a slim but muscular body. He was smiling widely at Patricia, at which Samuel pulled her closer still, ignoring the puzzled look that Dominic aimed in his direction.

"Patricia, I would like to introduce you to our distant cousin, Frederick. He was born in Amsterdam. I seem to recall a cousin making a new life over there when I was younger, but they lost touch with the family," Enid said, looking delightedly at the newcomer.

Patricia dipped her head in acknowledgement of Frederick's deep bow. When it seemed that Enid was not going to introduce Samuel, he took matters into his own hands and held out his hand.

"Earl of Bentham and the fiancé to your new cousin," he said with a pointed glance at Enid. He could tell she was unhappy with his possessive-sounding statement, but she managed to hold her counsel.

"Pleased to meet you, my lord. Frederick Heller at your service." Frederick turned his attention back to Patricia. "Would you do me the honour of having the next dance with me if you are not already taken?"

Samuel's fingers unconsciously dug into Patricia's side, making her release a squeak of protest. She quickly tried to pass it off as a cough, then smiled.

"Of course, that would be delightful and the perfect opportunity for me to ask you lots of questions. I had never heard of any relatives settling abroad before today; there is no mention of it in the family Bible," she said of the large tome within which family members painstakingly kept a record of everyone related to them. "Perhaps they were running away from a scandal."

Frederick looked a little taken aback at Patricia's words, at which Samuel smiled. "And have been cast off as reprobates," he continued, encouraging her.

Patricia grinned at him. "I knew my family could not be so staid and boring as it has been made out. At last, there is hope for some wrongdoing to be discovered."

"Patricia! Mind your tongue!" Enid scolded.

"Sorry," she said, completely unrepentant.

In plenty of time for the next dance, the group returned to the ballroom. Patricia had elbowed Samuel in the ribs when he had uttered 'coxcomb' at Frederick's chatter before putting some distance between them. They might be engaged, but being so close would still shock the wider gathering.

She smiled at him as they stood at the edge of the ballroom. "The dance will be a perfect way to show off the beautiful present you have given me." She touched the necklace briefly. "I am vain enough to want people to consider that it enhances my looks."

"You do not need trinkets to enhance you in any way. You are fine just the way you are," Samuel ground out.

Patricia looked lost for words at his statement, but it was Frederick who broke the silence. "Those are not very good words for a man in love," he scolded Samuel. "Fine is not a compliment to such a beautiful creature."

Samuel rolled his eyes and did not try to hide it. "As we have known each other for years, my fiancée knows exactly how I feel about her."

Patricia did not necessarily agree with Samuel's words, for she had spent the last few days in complete confusion, but knew by the set of his face that he would continue to argue with Frederick if she did not do something to divert the situation.

"The dancers are gathering. Should we join them?" she asked Frederick, who replied with yet another deep bow and held out his hand to lead her to the line that was rapidly forming.

"How in God's name did you find him?" Dominic asked his grandmother when Frederick was out of earshot.

"Mind your tongue," Enid said. "He begged forgiveness but introduced himself, saying that someone had pointed me out to him."

"Rude that he did not wait to be introduced," Dominic said, making Samuel even more grateful for his friend than he was already.

"Not when he is family, it isn't," Enid responded.

"A family member we did not know of until this evening," Dominic pointed out.

"What does it matter? We know about the connection now, and the timing could not be better. Excuse me, I want to ask Richard how Marie is doing," she said of her friend, who was Richard's aunt.

"Why does she dislike you so much?" Dominic asked in amusement. "She has never shown any animosity towards you before."

"Take your pick. It could be the fact that I am the worst kind of rake, who has no scruples, and who should have been beaten often as a child to improve the adult I have become. Or my suspicion that it is to do with the fact that if Patricia marries, there is no one else to look after her in her dotage."

"No! Really? But that does not explain why she would encourage another."

"Perhaps she thinks a family member will let her reside with them?"

"I suppose it could be that."

"And who says I would not do the same?"

"You actually have to ask that question? It might have something to do with you being the least family-oriented person I know."

The words were said in jest, but Samuel felt them as if he had been punched. For as far back as he could remember, he had longed to be part of a loving family. It was only that to try and attain that, he would have to open himself up to trust someone, which would inevitably be misplaced, leading to further hurt. He would not allow himself to be so vulnerable, no matter how intense the longing became.

"You would be surprised," he said gruffly.

"Patricia is going to win the bet then?"

"Hardly," he scoffed.

"Look on the positive side. At least Grandmamma will be happy when Patricia supposedly breaks the engagement. Poor Grandmam-ma, she would be in whoops if she knew the truth."

"Do not be tempted to tell her," Samuel said.

"Not I," Dominic responded. "I am just going to stand by and watch the situation unfold because, for whatever reason, she has decided she dislikes this engagement. She is clearly going to try and get Patricia to change her mind and make a match of it with this new cousin. I said from the start she was up to something, and I am now even more convinced of it. She was determined to marry Patricia off when they attended the house party the other month, so it seems she simply dislikes you, rather than the married state. I will be standing and watching with amusement as she tortures you. She can be a wily creature when she chooses to be."

"Go to the devil," Samuel muttered, making Dominic laugh.

"What do you think of our so-called cousin? Could he be our thief?"

Samuel was amused that Dominic was considering possible cul-prits, just as he had when he assessed who was in attendance. It was a strange and unusual feeling to be able to talk to people about what he was working on. True, he could have strangled Patricia when she had initially taken others into her confidence, but he had to acknowledge that there were advantages to it now that he could discuss the situation with his friends.

"I would be surprised if he has anything to do with the thefts," he said quietly, checking to make sure no one was in earshot. "If he has only just come into society, he will not have had the opportunity to carry out any earlier thievery."

"True, but he seems a slippery devil," Dominic said.

"I agree, there does seem something amiss with him. It is all too convenient that he suddenly appears and is so perfect—in your grandmother's opinion anyway."

Dominic laughed. "She seems smitten. I hope we find out more about him before he manages to wangle his way further into grand-mamma's good books."

Samuel smiled before glancing at Patricia, which made the smile fall from his face. "Whoever or whatever he is, he is able to make your sister laugh."

"You are acting the jealous lover to perfection." Dominic grinned at his friend.

"Humph," Samuel responded, never taking his eyes off Patricia, refusing to acknowledge that Dominic's words were far closer to the truth than he would like to admit.

Chapter Five

FREDERICK WAS INDEED making Patricia laugh, but Samuel would have been reassured to know that it was not because she was in any way smitten with him. His over-the-top gestures and words made her agree with Samuel's description of him. She thought him harmless enough, and she was interested to find out more about him, not for any other reason but curiosity.

"Tell me about your family," she said when he had stopped telling her how wonderful she looked, how lucky Samuel was, and how he wished he had known her before she had become attached. They were ridiculously forward words on such a short acquaintance, but she had laughed, not taking them seriously.

"Ah, it is a sad story. There was a race to get married and then a disinheritance. My grandfather was good in business and decided that Amsterdam was the place to make his fortune," Frederick explained as they danced. "He would have been upset to see the new ruler take over," he said of Napoleon's brother, who now controlled the country.

"It is so sad to hear what is happening on the Continent."

"I decided I could stand it no longer and would try and find my family in England if there were any I could trace. I am delighted that I have managed to find you so soon."

"There are not many of us," Patricia said as they moved down the line. "Just another cousin in Yorkshire, but we rarely see her. How long have you been over here?"

"A few weeks. I have a friend who introduced me to some families who were kind enough to invite me to their parties, and through speaking to others, I heard about you. I wanted to meet you immediately, I was so excited, but it seemed you were away from London for some time?"

"We recently attended a house party and then have been a little quieter than usual," Patricia said.

"But tonight we meet, and I am so happy!"

"Do you have other family? Are there more cousins?"

"No," Frederick answered shortly. "There is just me."

Patricia did not believe what he said. His smile had slipped somewhat, and she wondered what reason he could have for not telling the truth, but she would watch and wait.

"I hope to see you often now that we have found each other," Frederick said, squeezing her hands as they turned.

"I am sure we will," Patricia said.

"Your grandmother speaks very highly of you, and I can see why. I am happier than I have been for a long time. I am besotted already." He kissed her hand, but Patricia pulled away in surprise.

"Cousin! Please!" she hissed at him. "I am a newly engaged woman; you should not be so inappropriate. It is wrong."

"But we are family!" Frederick responded, eyes wide in surprise.

"No one knows that yet. I would beg you to be more circumspect with your grand gestures and flowery words."

"My apologies." He bowed his head. "I am sorry."

"It is fine. There are clearly differences in our countries, but I urge you not to do anything like that again." Patricia detected a flicker of something in his eyes as she berated him. Was it annoyance? She did not know him well enough to be sure, but she was certainly not impressed with his actions.

"You have my word as a gentleman and your cousin." Frederick bowed as the dance ended.

"Thank you."

Patricia had not waited for Frederick to escort her back to their group, but turned and walked away, wishing to put some distance between them. She had been polite in dancing with him, but she was not going to spend the rest of the evening in his company, cousin or not. As she moved through the throng of people, a woman charged into her, painfully knocking her shoulder.

"Oww!" Patricia exclaimed.

"Oh, I beg pardon," the woman said with a sneer.

"Have I done something to upset you? That was a deliberate attack and an unnecessary one from my perspective," Patricia asked, rubbing her shoulder.

"You have not, but I want to give you a friendly warning."

"Oh really? So far, your actions have been anything but pleasant. What piece of advice are you so eager to share?"

"I would not order your wedding trousseau anytime soon. He will tire of you before too long. It is what he does," she said.

Having looked closer at the woman, she now recognised her as one of the widows who had been pointed out as one of Samuel's previous conquests. "Ah, I thought I had seen you before," Patricia said. "You should learn to accept defeat gracefully. Being spiteful does you no credit."

The woman looked surprised at Patricia's calm response. "You will not capture him. You are an innocent. A man like his lordship needs a woman who can satisfy him."

"It would appear not, as he tired of you." Patricia shrugged and then winced at the throbbing in her shoulder.

"You..."

"Is there a problem, cousin?" Frederick asked, but Patricia looked over his shoulder and saw Samuel bearing down on them, glower firmly in place.

"I am fine, thank you," she said to Frederick. "My lord, your timing is perfect. I am in need of refreshment." She moved around Frederick and slipped her arm through Samuel's.

He did not respond to her but turned to the woman who was staring at him. "You have no business with my betrothed," he snapped, ignoring the flicker of pain that crossed her face at his words.

"I was telling her the reality of being with you and how it would never last," she said, trying to sound defiant, but her voice wobbled.

"Did you suggest that she might wish to pretend to be increasing in order to trap me into marriage? Miss Leaver would never stoop so low as to try such a cruel trick."

The woman flushed. "I thought I was."

"Rubbish! There was never a chance, and we both knew it. I thought we had been honest with each other from the start. It was you who changed the arrangement we had, not I, and I ensured you would not be out of pocket when things came to an end. You helped to convince me that I need to look at my life seriously and marry someone I could trust. Come, my love, we do not have to stay and listen to this nonsense."

"I see your trinkets have improved over the years," the woman cried as a parting shot. "When he is sick of you, those will cease to be given."

"I shall keep that in mind. In future, I will just ask for the more expensive ones so I can sell them if he deserts me. In the meantime, I will be sleeping with this beautiful necklace by my side, for I would not wish to lose something so precious. Is it not wonderful that my beloved has given me such a fine piece of jewellery—one bestowed on the family by the Queen—as an engagement present. I feel very lucky indeed."

"Enjoy it while you can. He will never commit to anyone," the woman snapped, able to sound stronger when looking at Patricia.

"If you say so," Patricia said, turning her back on the woman and pulling Samuel away before he could respond. "It is not worth causing a scene. People are already listening," she whispered.

Samuel said nothing until they were in the refreshment room, and he had drunk two glasses of wine in quick succession. "I am sorry," he said, finally breaking the silence between them.

"What for? You did nothing wrong. In fact, you came to my rescue at just the right moment." Patricia sipped her own drink, aware that Samuel was struggling with what had happened.

"I put you in the situation where women like her would think it perfectly reasonable to attack you and speak to you with such impropriety." Samuel was furious with himself, with his past actions and, more worryingly, with the opinion Patricia must now have of him.

"If I am honest, I feel a little sorry for her, though I wish she had been gentler with her method of introduction," she said with a roll of her shoulder.

"You feel sorry for her? I suppose I may sound a brute, but I am always honest before starting any relationship." The sinking feeling in his stomach surprised him. Did she no longer think so highly of him because of his past? He sincerely hoped that was not the case.

For some time, his annoyance at being considered a shallow rake—as everyone viewed him—was growing. He inwardly cursed himself. In reality, the only person he wanted to look at him with respect was Patricia and she knew far too much about his past to be able to put it out of her mind. It was a sad thought that she did not always see the best of him.

"Both of you were naïve to think there was no risk of one of you becoming more attached than the other. You say I am a green girl, but if you believe that no one would fall in love with you, happy to just have a dalliance, then you, my dear friend, are a Johnny Raw." Patricia laughed at the expression on Samuel's face. "Oh, come now, tell me you did not believe the words you uttered to every mistress you ever had, for from what I have witnessed of their remorse once you have left them behind, they clearly did not."

"I truly never set out to hurt anyone."

"I believe you, but you did not understand how your attentions would affect them. You are considered quite a catch, you know."

"My title and fortune are."

"There is more to it than that, but yes, those have a huge draw. You were not thinking straight with the type of women you were…spending time with. You should have chosen an actress or opera singer; they would have lower expectations."

"Good God! You are a revelation indeed. You have managed to shock and impress me in equal measure."

"I will take that as a compliment, but still, I feel sorry for her. She has lost you and is not getting any younger. I do think it foolish of widows to think they can persuade a younger man to marry them and not consider the fact that the same man might just be enjoying his freedom until he finds his true love or a suitable match with a large dowry," Patricia said.

"You seem to have studied the situation in great detail."

"I have observed that a large dowry can make the plainest of young ladies beautiful and her annoying habits endearing. It is sometimes quite a revelation what can be overcome in the pursuit of a profitable match. It would not surprise me if a hunched-back, bald, one-legged termagant was considered a diamond of the season if she had twenty thousand a year to soften the blow." Her words were meant to get a reaction out of Samuel, and she smiled when he threw his head back and laughed.

"You little minx!" he spluttered. "It is a good thing Dominic is not around to hear this, or he would lock you in your chamber and never let you out."

"He could not. It is by listening to Dominic that I know so much," Patricia said archly.

They heard the announcement that the waltz was the next dance, and Samuel held out his hand. "Come, my delight. I wish to dance with you and to show everyone I am in earnest this time."

Patricia put her hand in his, the inner warmth she had felt when teasing him out of his doldrums making her smile. She was grateful she seemed to know how to bring a lightness to him. She had an almost innate need to see him happy, for he had spent so much of his time troubled. To give him credit, he was as receptive to her needs as she was to him. It was a bond they shared.

Then reality set in to her happy thoughts. They were playing a role, nothing more than acting a part, and she would do well to remember that. This increased level of familiarity was not real, she repeated to herself as they returned to the ballroom.

Samuel twirled her into his arms when they reached the dance floor, making her laugh once more, but as soon as the music started, Patricia had to do something to keep herself focused, or her thoughts would wander to unsafe areas, thanks to their close proximity.

He was such a handsome man, but it was not just his looks that attracted her. The man she knew was a good friend, a principled man. Though he had been unwise with his dalliances—as most young men where—there was a major difference between him and others in his situation. He cared about issues, despite the public persona he wore. She had always thought highly of him, then as she had grown, she had had to acknowledge that her feelings for him had grown deeper. Now they were acting the part of a happy couple, it was harder to separate reality from fantasy. But it would not be a happy ending for her if she did not take control of her emotions.

"I think I should start to invite you to spend some time with those who I think would be a suitable wife," she said, trying to ignore the fact that he moved with surprising grace, holding her as if she was some precious object and making her insides spin when he looked at her intensely, as he was doing now. She had danced with him many times before, but had never felt as much or been affected by his closeness, the way she was now. She needed all her wits about her to remain focused.

"You want to start now? Are you so desperate for a necklace?"

Patricia was not quite convinced of the teasing tone in his voice and wondered if she had upset him. "I know you agreed to only start after we have solved the mystery," she said, being cautious with her words. "But do you not think it would be a perfect opportunity to meet potential candidates without any pressure on either side?"

"You seem to have everything worked out to perfection," was his stiff response.

"Oh, come on! You know you need to marry at some point. It might as well be to someone we all like. I would hate to think of you married to a woman who disliked Dominic's and my friendship with you."

"That would be reason enough for the marriage not to go ahead."

"I agree." Patricia smiled. "Which is why it is vital that we find you someone perfect."

"There is no such thing as a perfect match."

Patricia rolled her eyes, which made Samuel smile. "Perfect for you then. Is that better?"

"A little."

They both fell silent as the dance continued. Patricia loved the fact that Samuel was a good head taller than her; she usually struggled with finding partners she did not dwarf.

When the dance came to an end, Samuel smiled at her. It was a tender look to which Patricia responded in kind. "Thank you for doing this. I really do appreciate it," he said sincerely.

"It is a good change, having something interesting to do."

His expression turning impassive, he offered his arm, and they returned to Enid and Frederick. When Frederick started babbling to Patricia once more, Samuel stood slightly to the side, watching the exchange but making no effort to involve himself. That he was worried about Frederick's attentions toward Patricia was not revealed, he embraced his detached air, falling back onto his tried and tested protections when feeling lost and out of his depth.

He would have been reassured to know that Patricia was as equally confused and torn as he was.

Chapter Six

"THERE IS NO way on this earth you can persuade me that you need to sleep in my sister's chamber," Dominic ground out when they had returned home and Enid had retired to bed.

"Keep your voice down, you fool!" Samuel snapped. "We do not know if servants are involved. Do you want to reveal everything? We have been spreading the story that the necklace belonged to the Queen and that Patricia is keeping it very close to her. We had to let that be known so that any attempt at the theft is directed to one place. I have to be inside the room in case they strike, or we will be no better off."

Dominic looked a little chastened but still shook his head. "I will not change my mind on this and do not even attempt to agree to it," he shot at Patricia.

"I would not dare," she said with some amusement, but she had been shocked when Samuel had told her that he needed to spend the night in her bedchamber.

"Patricia will sleep in a guest chamber and I will be in hers alone. But we can only accomplish this when the servants have gone to bed. I will have disappeared before they rise in the morning," he said, then turned to Patricia, "though it will mean that you need to be awake very early, before anyone else rises."

"I am sure I will survive the hardship," she said.

"And how do we explain the use of a guest chamber?" Dominic demanded.

"I am capable of making a bed," Patricia said.

"This plan keeps getting worse," Dominic muttered.

"If you think leaving Patricia in her chamber is a better idea, then you are not as intelligent as you make out."

"Comments like that will result in a bloodied nose for you, my friend."

Samuel smiled. "That is more like it. I know this is far from ideal, but my first priority is to protect Patricia in all of this."

"And if you are seen leaving the house in the early morning, that will not have any effect at all," Dominic said sarcastically.

"I can get in and out of here unseen by anyone."

"Except the one time you are seen. You do not know this household and could make a mistake."

"I promise to do everything in my power to not be discovered," Samuel said. "I need to be where the necklace is, or we will be chasing the thief after the event. That has not worked in the past."

"It is a hell of a risk for Patricia."

"I know."

"Are you both prepared to be forced into a real marriage if you are discovered? For that will be the result," Dominic said.

Samuel looked at Patricia. "I would hate to force you into something you would hate, but Dominic is right. If I get caught…"

"It is the only way. We are too far in to back out now. I accept the risk and if we have to marry—" She shrugged her shoulders. She could not admit—even to herself—that would be a dream come true. But it would be the worst start to a marriage that anyone could have. The thought that Samuel would resent her if he was forced into matrimony almost made her call a halt to the whole scheme. But she could not let him down.

"Yet again, I wish to register that I do not like this," Dominic said.

"I know, but Samuel has given us his word, and that should be good enough."

Samuel smiled at her words. "Thank you."

"You are welcome. Now it is time I was asleep. I will get undressed in my room and then dismiss Jess. When she has gone, I will move to the blue room; it is the closest to my own."

"Good night, Patricia, and once again, thank you for taking everything in stride," Samuel said, standing while she left the room.

Dominic shot him a glare. "If anything happens untoward…"

"You will not punish me as much as I will myself," Samuel said quietly.

Dominic did not seem reassured but stood. "I will go and dismiss the servants; there should only be my valet about. Give it half an hour, and then the house should be clear."

Samuel nodded, and Dominic left him alone in the room, closing the door behind him. Blowing out all but one candle, Samuel sat, staring into the fire. He was not afraid of confronting a thief, but he was perturbed at the thought of spending the night in Patricia's room. The idea of being surrounded by her things, of sitting on the bed she slept in, made him ache for more from her. It was unfair and stupid of him to think in such a way when she had made it plain that she was still intent on finding him a wife. The best thing he could do was throw himself into her scheme and try to forget his body's reaction when he had held her for the waltz.

Sighing, he looked at his pocket watch. It would be a long night. And there was something that neither of his friends had realised in all of this—and there was no way in hell he was going to tell Dominic, though it made him the worst kind of cad.

He would be the one to wake Patricia.

PATRICIA AWOKE WITH a start when someone shook her gently. Hearing the 'shh' which followed the shake, she seemed to blink herself awake. "Samuel?"

"Yes, I am departing now," he whispered.

"The thief?"

"No sight or sound, unfortunately. Can I do the same tonight? I know it is an imposition on you." He was stroking her arm, had not been able to remove his hand after gently shaking her. Never having seen her with her hair down, he had touched it reverently to move it away from her shoulder so he could awaken her. Looking at him sleepily through half-closed eyes, she had never been so appealing.

"It is fine. We can do whatever is needed." She yawned. "You must be shattered."

He smiled at her concern. "I will not be around much in the mornings until this is over."

"I am to be neglected by my future husband."

"I promise to make it up to you." Acting on impulse, he bent over and planted a kiss on her head. "I must go. Goodbye."

Patricia watched him leave before swinging her legs off the bed and, once standing, started to straighten the covers. The exchange had been intimate even before the kiss, confusing her further, but for the moment at least, she was too tired to think about the way her long-time friend was now affecting her.

When she returned to her own chamber, the curtains were around the bed, but when she pulled one back, the covers were untouched, apart from a slight dip on top of them. He had clearly not slept in her bed, something she was both relieved and disappointed about at the same time. Pulling the covers over her head, she sighed, letting tiredness wash over her, and fell into a sleep filled with dreams of kisses and closeness to a man she could not have.

A FEW DAYS after the ball, they all went to watch a play. Samuel had booked a box and had reluctantly invited Frederick. Dominic had said he would be bringing a friend, and Enid had brought one as well. With Isabelle and Sophia joining them, they were a large group, and Patricia hoped that the evening would help to settle her confusing thoughts and feelings.

When Dominic entered the room with a woman Patricia had never met before, she looked at her with undisguised interest. Dominic had never brought anyone to a gathering. The stranger was willowy with dark hair and even darker eyes. Patricia wondered if she had some foreign blood, the olive of her skin enhancing her beauty further.

Dominic ignored the look of curiosity Enid sent him at his entrance, but instead approached Patricia. "Juliet, please let me introduce my sister to you. Patricia, this is Miss Juliet Barbosa."

"I am pleased to meet you, Miss Leaver. Your brother speaks highly of you," Juliet said.

"As all good brothers should." Patricia smiled. "I am pleased to make your acquaintance. Have you been in London long?"

Juliet smiled. "It is not my first time in London, but this time I have only been here a few weeks. The city is lively, and I enjoy my time here, but it is much colder than it is at home."

"And where is home?"

"Portugal, though I have moved around a lot. My father is involved with the shipping trade and has many ships."

"It sounds like a very interesting life. Oh, please allow me to introduce my betrothed to you."

When the introductions were made, Samuel started to speak Portuguese to Juliet, and though Patricia sent him a look of surprise, she took the opportunity of stepping away a little to speak to Dominic.

"This is a surprise."

"I have been waiting for the right moment to introduce her to you. Isn't she beautiful?"

"She certainly is," Patricia acknowledged. "How long have you known her? It is most unlike you to keep secrets."

Dominic gave a rueful laugh. "Only since Amelia's ball, but I am not afraid to say that I have never felt this strongly about anyone before. I know it is early, probably far too early to be uttering anything like this, but this is it for me. She is the one."

"That is very sudden. Are you sure it is wise to make a decision so life-changing, so quickly?"

"The moment I saw her, I was lost. I cannot bear to be apart from her."

Patricia did not respond immediately. She was astonished to hear Dominic gush over a woman so early in his acquaintance with her. "Have you met her family?" she asked.

"Of course! I am smitten, not stupid."

"I never said you were."

"You did not need to. To put your mind at rest, yes, I have met her family…well to be fair, just her father. Her mother is still in Portugal with a sister, but her father welcomed me from the first. He is a little brusque and looks the part of a sailor with his ruddy complexion, but he had many interesting stories about sailing, which he was happy to share. I think they have been all over the world."

Patricia looked behind him with a knowing look, then chuckled. "Here comes Grandmamma."

"I am impressed it has taken her this long," Dominic whispered before smiling at Enid. "Come and meet my gorgeous girl," he said.

"I cannot wait," Enid responded.

Frederick had approached Patricia when Dominic had moved to interrupt the conversation between Samuel and Juliet. "Your brother has a good eye for beauty, but she cannot compare to you, my cousin."

"Now that is a bit too brown!" Patricia exclaimed on a laugh. "I am well aware of my own limitations, and I do not see any point in trying to compare myself to someone like Miss Barbosa."

"I see no reason why not. I know that I am determined to look for my own English rose, for there is nothing so beautiful."

"This particular rose is taken," Samuel said, taking hold of Patricia's hand and kissing it, looking into her eyes with a tender smile.

"You do have the habit of appearing at the wrong moment, my lord." Frederick had lost the happy expression he always cultivated around Patricia and was openly scowling at Samuel.

"As this is my box and my betrothed you are making flowery speeches to, *my* betrothed and I would suggest you remember that, or I might just have to bring the message home another way. But in this instance, I would say that my timing is perfect." There was a smoothness to Samuel's words, but it was clear he was issuing a warning to the newcomer.

"You are a suggesting I am being unscrupulous?"

"Are you?"

"I am being friendly to my new cousin, whom I consider to be a diamond."

"Then that is one area we can agree on. She is indeed a diamond and very precious to me. And I will not leave her open to censure because another is behaving in an inappropriate way towards her."

"She can spend time with whomever she wishes. And I am family. There is no scandal to be afraid of."

"There had better not be, for I will not stand by while you put my beloved at risk. Take my words as you wish, but be assured that I am perfectly serious."

Frederick stood tall, as if preparing to attack or some other foolhardy attempt to get the better of Samuel before moving away without another word.

"I do not think your cousin is fond of me," Samuel said.

"I wonder why that is? You had no need to worry, though. When he tried to compare me to Miss Barbosa, I lost all patience with him," Patricia said.

"I am not surprised, for you are far preferable to a woman who is keen to speak of money and wealth the moment she is introduced. It is not appropriate conversation with a new acquaintance. As well, I found her use of language to be very interesting."

Patricia had reacted with a roll of her eyes at Samuel's first words, but curiosity got the better of her. "What nuggets of information did you glean from her? I was quite impressed with your ability to speak Portuguese."

"There is a lot about me to be impressed by."

Patricia laughed. "Stop trying to be a man of mystery and tell me what you found out. Dominic claims to be head over heels for her, so I need to know as much as I can."

"You certainly know how to destroy a man."

"Hardly! That self-assuredness you have can only be shaken by an earthquake, and I am not even sure it would falter then."

It was Samuel's turn to roll his eyes, but before Patricia could insult him further, he decided to answer her question. "I did not find out much. She has visited many places but is looking to settle. She made a point of saying that she did not need a rich husband, for her father was looking to buy an estate and give it to her as a wedding present."

"If I were her, I would not let Dominic hear her uttering those words."

"Why not? Would it not make her even more of an attractive option?"

"You know how he is about not acknowledging that we are far from wealthy. And if it becomes common knowledge that she has beauty *and* wealth, it will not be long before there is a line of potential suitors banging on her door."

"You think she could be swayed towards someone else so easily? That would suggest a major weakness in her character. I would hate to see Dominic hurt in such a way, if he has indeed lost his heart."

Patricia placed her hand on Samuel's arm and squeezed it, knowing that it was his own experiences with an unhappy marriage—in this case, his parents'—that increased his concern for Dominic. His father had been hurt so much, yet still professed to be in love with his mother. Witnessing their one-sided marriage had shown Samuel the dangers of giving his heart. She ached that he had not experienced a happy childhood. Patricia might have lost her parents at a young age, but she had always been surrounded by family members who loved and respected each other.

"I have no idea about her character. You have conversed with her for far longer than I have. I just know the way people view wealth. That she is beautiful, too, only adds to the attraction. I hope she is as attached to Dominic as he seems to her, but if not, I would rather him find out before they are wed than after."

"It would be wise to keep an eye on things. A couple of times, she piqued my attention as we spoke," Samuel said.

"In what way?"

"I slipped a few Spanish words into the conversation, and she did not react nor tease me about my faults or lack of finesse with my abilities with her mother tongue."

"I do not think that is anything to be suspicious over. Spanish and Portuguese are similar languages, are they not?"

"I would not admit that to either native of their country." Samuel smiled at her.

"Good point. I will view her as I would any new acquaintance. I will speak up if there is something amiss, but if we start looking for faults, we are sure to find them."

Samuel squeezed her hand, which was still resting on his arm, some of the tension leaving his face. "As always, you are correct. I should learn to listen to you more."

"That, my dear friend, is music to my ears."

"Friend?" Enid asked, suddenly appearing behind them. "That is a strange term for you to use, Patricia."

"Not at all. We have been firm friends for years," Samuel answered without hesitation. "To be friends as well as husband and wife is a clear sign that we are set for a strong and happy marriage."

Patricia nodded in agreement, unsure that she had looked convincing enough with the sharp look Enid sent her, but there was nothing she could do about it now. Thankfully, the first act of the play started, and the party sat down, preventing further conversation.

Chapter Seven

PATRICIA WAS AWAKENED by a gentle shake but groaned and tried to slap away the hand, causing Samuel to chuckle. "Come on, sleepy head. It is time to change rooms."

"I'm so comfortable."

"You look it," Samuel acknowledged. He brushed her hair away from her face. It was wrong—he was being unfair to them both—but he could not resist the urge to touch her.

"I will say I walk in my sleep," she mumbled.

"And have your grandmother taking you to every doctor within twenty miles because she is worried about you?"

Patricia groaned. "You are mean."

"I promise I will make it up to you."

"I do not see what could be more tempting than snuggling under these covers."

"Good grief, Patricia, you do know how to torment a man."

The words had her opening her eyes in confusion. "I do not understand."

"Good," he said. Kissing her head as he had the previous mornings, he let his lips linger a moment longer than before. "You are even more beautiful first thing in the morning than you are the rest of the day. It is unfair of me to admit, but I am glad I am the only one to have seen your rumpled state."

Patricia was staring at him wide-eyed, making Samuel aware of what he was saying. "Ignore me," he said quickly, moving to the door. "I am tired from sitting up all night to no avail. That blasted thief is proving hard to entice. I would have thought there would have been an attempt by now but the necklace is still in place and I am left uttering nonsense as a result. Good day, Patricia."

He closed the door before Patricia could answer him, and he was thankful. Hurrying to put some space between them, he had to force himself not to break out into a run, his urge to escape was so great. Sound would bring attention to him, and he had to concentrate on making a quiet escape, or there would be even more issues to contend with.

When away from the house and no longer in danger of discovery, he took a deep breath. His heart was pounding, and it had had nothing to do with the risk of discovery.

What the devil had he done? He had persuaded her to join him in a situation which he should never have even considered. He had thought of her the moment he needed help. He could try to convince himself that it was because of their long-time friendship, but now, he realised it was more than that. His own need to gain approval from the Regent and the Queen had made him desperate, prepared to do anything, even involve Patricia. He was as selfish as his mother was.

Since this case had started, he had not been acting. He was happy to be engaged to her. He wanted to be, damn it. The main problem was she was still talking about finding him a wife, clearly seeing him as nothing but a friend. So far, she had not done anything about it. And though he wanted to imagine that she had changed her mind—that she felt the same way he did—he knew it was wishful thinking. Admittedly, she had reacted to him occasionally, but those had been the actions of an innocent being swept away in the moment. He, though, was far from innocent and had never felt this way about anyone before. It terrified him.

Taking off his stovepipe hat, he ran his hand through his hair. He had never intended to fall in love, but he had. He wondered how long he had felt this way about Patricia, for it was clear he had not suddenly developed feelings for her, but this closeness they were experiencing had brought his true emotions to the fore.

The question was, what was he going to do with this new knowledge? How the devil was he going to confess all to her and then, even more worrying, admit the truth to Dominic?

If he revealed the depth of his affection, he risked losing the two people who meant the most to him. That was a risk he could not bear to take, not right now. He had never felt so accepted or welcomed by anyone else, but if he decided not to speak, then he would never be able to touch her, kiss her, tease her in the ways he longed to. Not sure that he could remain near her if she ever found a husband, he struggled with the sobering thought that no matter what happened, he was going to lose her.

As one not used to having such a cacophony of confusing feelings, he struggled to see a way through them. But he knew one thing—they would not go away anytime soon.

PATRICIA FELT OUT of sorts after Samuel's visit and welcomed her friends at the end of morning calls with more outward enthusiasm than she normally would display. Relieved to have her mind distracted from what had happened that morning, she set about enjoying their company.

"I feel I have not had the chance to speak to you without someone disturbing us for far too long," she said as she handed out cups of tea to them all.

"I think it is more to do with the fact that you spend your time gazing into Lord Bentham's eyes," Sophia said, all amusement.

"I do not!"

"Oh, I am not saying that he is not doing exactly the same in return," Sophia defended her words. "In fact, I hope that one day someone will look at me the way he looks longingly at you."

"I have seen people trying to speak to him, and he has been so distracted, watching you, that they have given up and walked away," Isabelle added.

"You know he is not the best in company. He is always like that," Patricia responded, inwardly allowing herself to be hopeful that Samuel might not be as indifferent to her as she feared, then as quickly cursing herself for her stupidity.

"He does gaze at you," Amelia said. "Richard has even commented on it. He begged me to tell him that he had not behaved in such a besotted way with me." The group laughed at her words.

"And what was your response?" Sophia asked.

"I could not tell him he was exactly as smitten as Lord Bentham is. He is still under the impression that he is considered one of the *ton* who is quick with a set-down and feared by the younger dandies. It would be cruel to tell him they consider him a man firmly leg-shackled and lost to them."

"Men can be so foolish sometimes," Isabelle said.

Amelia grinned. "But we love them."

Patricia thought it prudent to change the subject and soon had everyone talking about what other scandals there were outside their circle. It was the perfect way to avert any further chatter about Samuel and her engagement. She knew she could not always avoid it, but it felt like a relief to pretend life was not complicated and she could laugh, eat cake and enjoy a real catch-up.

Eventually it was time to disperse, and Sophia and Isabelle set off together, leaving Amelia as she had made an excuse to remain behind. As soon as they heard the front door close, Amelia started to speak.

"I know we were teasing you somewhat, but all that was said was true. What is happening between you two? This no longer seems like it is an act for either of you."

Patricia slumped in her seat. "I have no idea. One thing is for certain, I never expected to feel like this. It scares me, for I have no clue as to what to do or what is happening. Whatever it is, it was not part of the plan."

"Why should it frighten you? Surely this makes things easier? You just marry after the thief has been apprehended."

"That is making the presumption that Samuel feels the same way about me as I do for him." She did not mention how he had been with her in the morning. She would be considered compromised with him being in her chamber, and rightly so. Though Amelia was her friend and she trusted her, she did not wish to see condemnation in her eyes if she confessed, and if Dominic became aware of what Samuel had done, there would be one horrific row. It added to her foolish thoughts, but she enjoyed that there were a few moments in which she had felt he cared for her. The feel of his hand on her shoulder and the way he gently touched her hair… It would take a harder person than Patricia to resist small flights of fancy at such actions.

"He is not indifferent to you. I know the reality of the situation, and I think he is besotted. No one can act so well, and everyone can see it; you are the talk of the *ton*, bringing such a confirmed bachelor to his knees."

"If only that were true."

"I think it is, and I am not just saying that because you are my friend and I want to see you happy. I can hardly believe the change in him, even since that first meeting when he walked in and discovered you had told me what you intended to do. Honestly, his demeanor towards you has dramatically shifted."

"He gives off confusing messages. One moment I am sure he feels something, the next, he is being formal and distant." She was glad to be able to voice some of her confusion; if she kept denying everything, it would sound as if she were fishing for compliments. "I never know which Samuel I am to be faced with, and it does not help that his whole manner can change from one sentence to the next."

"It sounds to me as if he is struggling as much as you are," Amelia said gently. "Isabelle is right that sometimes men can act strangely by ignoring what is blatantly obvious in front of them or even pushing aside what they are feeling. Richard struggled with accepting what he felt for me, although I was experiencing an equal torment."

"I thought a solution might be to start encouraging suitable women to spend more time in our company."

"Of all the actions you could choose to get him to see you are the one for him, why on earth would you do that? You should be encouraging his more tender feelings, not pushing him toward someone else."

"It will give him the opportunity of escape. I do want him to be happy—I always have—even if it does not include me." Her reasoning sounded hollow to her own ears; the only part said with any conviction was about his happiness.

"If you want to see him making pretty to someone else, go ahead. But believe me when I say it will feel like your heart is being cut in half. I had never experienced pain and despair like it."

"Was it so bad with Mrs. Grandison?" There was no need to ask what Amelia was referring to. She had endured a difficult time at the start of her marriage, believing her husband to be still in love with the woman who had jilted him. It was exacerbated by the fact the woman almost ran free over Richard's home. Finally, Amelia put her foot down, taking the situation in hand and happily discovering that her husband not only did not love Mrs. Grandison, but was deeply in love with Amelia.

"It was a nightmare of a time," Amelia said. "I still have the occasional horrible dream about it and would hate to see anyone I cared about going through anything similar. I am not being dramatic when I say it was the worst time of my life, and I include the accident in that.

Nothing can prepare you for loving someone and seeing them with someone else."

Patricia knew how hard life had been for Amelia after she had been attacked by a horse and thought never to walk again, so she took her friend's words seriously. "I cannot see a way around it. He needs someone special, someone who will love him as he deserves. Once I break off the engagement, we will not have any contact, at least for a while. Is it so wrong to need to know that he will be happy?"

"He would be happy with you!" Amelia said, exasperated. "I do not know why you are maintaining this defeatist attitude. I can only hope that he steps up to the mark and does something to convince you that there is no one he would rather be with, which is the way he feels, if his expressions are anything to go by."

"You are noticing things that are just the effect of us being close friends for years; you said yourself that society had not seen us together. Now you can see the easy way we are when we are in each other's company."

Amelia shook her head and stood up. "I will leave you now before I am tempted to shake some sense into you."

Patricia laughed. "I admit, I am not sorry you are leaving before you take such drastic action."

"Just promise me you will truly open your eyes and see what is plain to everyone else."

"I will try, but I think you are mistaken."

"I suppose trying is a start."

IT WAS HOURS later when Dominic entered the drawing room with Samuel. Patricia had been trying to concentrate on some needlework but was not making much progress. She was glad that Enid had retired for an afternoon nap, for she would have certainly noticed something was amiss with her. Her grandmother was one who would not rest until she had gotten to the bottom of an issue, and Patricia would not have been able to successfully deflect any questions in her current state of mind.

Samuel immediately approached her and bowed over her hand. "That poor piece of fabric looks to have been battered."

Patricia looked down with a grimace at the crumpled, badly stitched sampler. "Not one of my finest creations."

"Luckily, you are perfect in every other way. That more than makes up for it."

"Please spare me," Dominic groaned.

Samuel smiled at his friend. "Just keeping in character."

Patricia was grateful that Samuel had turned away, for he would have seen her disappointment before she managed to school her features so as not to betray her feelings.

"To what do I owe the pleasure?" she asked.

"I saw Samuel in White's and told him we need to bring this to a head. We cannot go on for weeks with him being here and all this sneaking around. The longer it takes for the thief to strike, the more likely it is that something will go wrong. It was not the best of plans to start with—there were too many things which could fall apart because of its simplicity."

"What are you proposing? Have you a plan?"

"Well, no," Dominic said. "But we thought we could talk it over."

"I would not wish to decide on a course of action without your input. You have been a vital part of this case," Samuel said to her.

"I am not sure what suggestion I could offer, apart from wearing the necklace again."

"There is the Thursby's ball this week. They are holding it on their estate near Ealing, and everyone will be attending," Dominic said. "The entertainments at their estates are always extravagant, not like their weekly gatherings in London."

"True, and in many cases, people will be staying over or nearby. Will you be staying in the house?" Samuel asked.

"Yes, Grandmamma is a close friend of theirs. Patricia might need to share a room, though," Dominic pointed out.

Samuel grimaced and turned to Patricia. "I will speak to Mrs. Thursby. She knew my father and has always had a soft spot for me. I'll beg her to allow you your own room, claiming that your grandmother is putting you under pressure not to marry me, but that we are determined to do so. I am sure she will support us. Would you be willing to wear the necklace again to reinforce how precious it is? The thief might not have wanted to breach this house, but if you are visiting someone else's estate, there is less opportunity of them being identified as a stranger," Samuel said.

"Of course, I am willing to do whatever is needed. As Dominic said, the sooner this is brought to a close, the better." Both men looked at her in surprise. Her tone had been overly sharp, but seeing him and feeling the way she did, made her feelings of confusion and uncertainty increase.

"Is your cousin invited?" Samuel asked Dominic.

"Why? Afraid of the competition?"

Samuel snorted, making Dominic laugh. "No, I just think it curious as to why he has suddenly appeared in company. And he has the perfect excuse to leave and return to the country without anyone thinking anything of it."

That Samuel was not being completely truthful about the reason he disliked the new arrival, he would never admit, but every time he saw the man fawn over Patricia, he was hit with a surge of jealousy. He could hardly warn Patricia off from speaking to him when there was supposedly a family connection—a convenient one, in Samuel's opinion—but he dreaded the moment Patricia ended their fake engagement, for without doubt, the blaggard would offer for her, he was sure of it.

"You did not believe me when I suggested he might be our thief. In fact, your reaction felt something akin to ridicule," Dominic said.

"I did not act any way of the sort, but I have had more time to consider it, and he does have the opportunity to get rid of the jewels."

"You cannot be serious." Patricia threw her needlework in the basket at her feet. "Just because you do not like him, that does not make him the thief. He hardly knows anyone. How could he have been gaining access to houses without detailed knowledge of the people who live there and the layout within?"

"I thought you were not keen on him?" Dominic asked.

"I am not, he is too…oh, I do not know how to describe it. He just seems too forward, too sure of himself. If he is who he claims to be, then it is wrong to be trying to fit him into being the thief when he could not possibly have been."

"He admits he has been in society for a while now, yet you were never introduced to him. He stated that he had heard about you, but he never sent a missive around to alert you of his presence. Is that not a little unusual?"

"We had some time away, did we not? At Mrs. Greenwood's house party. Because of what happened with her son, the party might have come to an abrupt end, but we remained with her after the guests had left. Grandmamma wanted to make sure Mrs. Greenwood was well. What her son did caused her a real shock."

"Yet your cousin did not visit the moment you returned to town. I would suggest it is because he has been out of the country."

Patricia glowered at Samuel. "You are not being impartial."

"Perhaps you are being too partial?" Samuel asked.

"Children! Children!" Dominic held his hands up to try to placate them both. "There is no need for this."

"Samuel is being a gudgeon. Frederick is perfectly pleasant." Patricia did not, and would not, admit that Samuel was right with regard to her cousin. His actions *were* a little odd. Still, it annoyed her that he seemed determined to dislike someone who was purporting to be interested in her. That she would never consider Frederick a suitable beau was irrelevant—it was an insult that Samuel thought anyone showing affection towards her had to have some sort of character deficiency. It hurt her more than she cared to admit, even to herself. She had always considered herself nothing out of the ordinary, but she had thought that Samuel had valued her. Unfortunately, it appeared not.

"It is a good thing you are not engaged in reality," Dominic said. "It would be a disaster." At his words, both Samuel and Patricia looked down, hiding their expressions and missing the knowing look Dominic wore. "Now we are over that little spat, we can prepare for the Thursby's ball. I think we need to offer more of an enticement for the thief."

"I am not putting Patricia at risk," Samuel immediately said, all anger towards her gone in his need to protect her.

"Of course not." Dominic did not try to hide his exasperation at his friend's presumption. "We need him to be tempted so much that he decides to act quickly."

Samuel nodded. "Reacting rather than planning increases the chances of mistakes being made."

"Precisely! I was thinking of letting it be known that Patricia is about to leave London."

"You have missed your calling. You should have joined Bow Street with Samuel," Patricia said.

"I might have done, if I had known about it." The pointed look he sent Samuel could not have been misunderstood.

"They approached me, not the other way around," Samuel defended himself. That he had found a role in which he felt he made a difference had been a happy accident. "If it makes you happy, I will put your name forward on my next visit."

"I would be grateful if you could."

"No!" Patricia almost shouted. "Worrying about one of you is bad enough. I don't want to worry about the safety of you both. No! That is too much." Dominic grinned at her, but Samuel wore one of his unreadable expressions.

"I still want to explore working with them," Dominic persisted.

"It is not all about putting ourselves in danger," Samuel tried to reassure her, but from the look on her face, he was not achieving his aim.

Not caring that Samuel probably thought her ridiculous, she lifted her chin and met his eyes. "It is the way I feel. I am bound to worry about you, whether you perceive there is danger or not. I refuse to be ashamed of caring."

"Quite so," came the quiet response, but he offered no other comment.

Chapter Eight

"WE NEED TO hold a dinner prior to the Thursby's ball," Enid said the following morning over breakfast. "We have had little time to get to know Juliet, and I think it is important that we make an effort."

"It would take some arranging," Dominic said.

"There is no need for a large gathering, say no more than thirty people," Enid continued. "I have some friends who are returned to London and have not met her."

"Will you be introducing Samuel to them?" Patricia asked.

"They already know him," Enid answered tartly. "I will have none of your sauce, young lady. I have already written to them of your engagement. They were as surprised as I was."

Patricia felt a trifle guilty at the response her outburst had caused and was immediately contrite. "I am sorry for sounding petulant. I just wish you welcomed Samuel as easily as you have Juliet."

Taking a sip of her tea, Enid watched Patricia over her cup. "When you are wed, I will welcome him with open arms as if he was my own. Until then…" She shrugged.

Patricia flushed and shot Dominic a panicked look but tried to remain passive—as much as she could with burning cheeks. "I will help you to prepare for the gathering," she said, changing the subject.

"Good, that is settled then. Dominic, check what day is best for Juliet."

"I can tell you now that Wednesday would be the best day for us. We were going to spend the evening together, but neither of us had any commitments to attend anything in particular," Dominic said.

"Wednesday it is then." Enid stood. "Finish your breakfast while I go and speak to Cook. We can send out invitations afterwards," she said to Patricia.

When Enid had left the room, Patricia leaned back in her chair. "She knows."

"She could be just being bloody-minded, which is unusual, I admit, but not unheard of," Dominic reasoned.

"No, she definitely knows something—or at least suspects things are not as they should be."

"I do not know how. The way you both act when together, you have convinced everyone, even those who were most sceptical about Samuel finally settling down."

"Except Grandmamma. She has been unconvinced from the start. I cannot believe it could be anything else. As Samuel has pointed out, she liked him well enough before we became engaged."

"I honestly do not know what else you could do to convince her." Dominic shrugged.

"I suppose, on a positive note, her being suspicious might mean that she will not react badly when it is time to call off the engagement."

Dominic laughed. "Keep believing that, dear sister. But I would wager that whether she believes you or not, she will still roast you."

"I think you might be right," Patricia groaned.

WEDNESDAY CAME AROUND amidst a flurry of activity. Though it was just a small gathering, Enid did not do things by halves. The dining room was adorned with floral displays around the outside, with smaller arrangements down the middle of the table intersected with candelabra. Enid was very sociable and enjoyed being able to see the whole of the table and keep an eye on all the people there. Only when she was perfectly satisfied that all was in order did she nod and retire upstairs to prepare for her guests.

Patricia dressed carefully for the evening. She was not wearing the jewels—they were to be worn at the Thursby's ball—but she'd donned a double row of pearls with matching earrings and bracelet. A pale blue dress with a sculpted neckline and puffed sleeves fitted her to perfection. A cream ribbon around her waist and cream gloves finished her outfit off. Her maid placed some carefully chosen flowers in her hair, setting off her dark curls to best advantage.

"You'll be the hit of the evening," the maid said, happy with her work.

"As the evening is being held to enable us to become more acquainted with Miss Barbosa, I think it is my role to fade into the background."

"Looking as well as you do, Miss Patricia, there is no chance of that. You've been glowing ever since you got engaged to his lordship."

Patricia gazed at her reflection in the looking glass. She could see a difference; she had been trying to ignore the fact, but the truth could not be avoided. She looked radiant, with a flush on her cheeks and a constant sparkle in her eyes. Never one for maudlin moods, she now felt as if she could not stop her smiles whenever she thought of being in Samuel's company. She was glad to be looking so well, but the temporary nature of their situation was always at the back of her mind. There would not be much to smile about when it was over.

Leaving her chamber and entering the drawing room, she was immediately approached by Samuel's mother. The Dowager Countess had remained on her sickbed for longer than was usual for her but had now decided that her son and his future wife needed her support.

"You look beautiful," she said, holding her hands out to Patricia and pulling her to her. She had never been a person to show any sort of emotion unless approached by a handsome man, so her actions took Patricia by surprise.

Patricia smiled but shot a look of appeal to Samuel. "Thank you."

"I have told Samuel that although he is my son, a daughter needs a mother when she is about to get married. He is old enough not to need my counsel, whereas you, my dear, have been motherless for a long time. Luckily, I will be delighted to step into the breach and be with you every step of the way." For a woman who had hardly ever shown any maternal feelings, this was completely out of character for her. Samuel's incredulous expression as he joined them let her know he was just as surprised.

Patricia was also insulted at the words on Enid's behalf. "My grandmamma has always done what she could to make up for the loss of my parents," she said stiffly.

"And I intend to continue doing so until I breathe my last," Enid responded tartly, appearing at Patricia's side. "What the devil are you up to, Imogen? You have never done an altruistic thing in your life. I do not see any reason for you to start now."

Samuel's mother looked fit to burst. "But you are not helping them. They have not even set a date for the wedding yet."

"Why are you so keen to see them married?" Enid asked.

"Then, perhaps, Samuel might no longer look at me with derision," she answered. "He will understand what marriage is really like, and when he is seeking solace elsewhere, I hope he will finally understand my motivation. There are more people in the world like me than like his father. He had many opportunities to seek entertainment elsewhere, yet it is I who is condemned, not of him. We would have been far happier if he had strayed, as you will find out, Samuel." The three of them stared at her in disbelief. "What? Is it wrong to want my son to like me?"

"Not at all," Enid answered. "But you could have achieved that by being a decent mother to him."

"I felt constrained by John. I wanted some happiness in my life," she said, unrepentantly.

"He never betrayed you the way you did him," Samuel ground out, fully aware that this was not the place for this conversation as they were attracting curious looks.

His mother waved his words away. "I never asked him to remain faithful. It was his choice."

"Mother…" Samuel warned.

"Stop being so prudish," his mother snapped at him.

Patricia placed her hand on Samuel's arm and squeezed. His muscles were tense beneath her touch. "Thank you for your offer. If we need any help, we will not hesitate to ask."

"I was only trying to assist. One moment I am being judged for being a bad parent, the next, I am insulted when I am only trying to make amends. I am willing to embrace this marriage, though my son's choice of bride comes with barely any dowry and nothing else of value." She looked at Patricia, her expression one of pity.

"Mother! Patricia is one of the finest people I have ever met. She is the woman I want, regardless of her looks or money," Samuel snapped, missing the look of horror on Patricia's face.

"Is it not? Let us see if you feel the same way after a few years of marriage and half a dozen children. When you are watching the fine young women smile at you, see if you do not give in to temptation."

"It is not a crime to admire others." Samuel did not see the damage his words were causing—not so much what his mother was saying, but what he was confirming.

"Imogen, you are a fool," Enid said, causing Imogen to turn on her heel and walk away.

"I am sorry," Samuel said to both Patricia and Enid. "It is often easier when she is indisposed. As she is ageing, she is definitely less careful about what she says or who she upsets."

"I do not know why people consider that you might not be your father's son. I think it more like he got some maid in the family way and told your mother she had to pretend you were hers," Enid said.

"Oh, if only," Samuel said.

"Now, let us not forget to compare your reputation to that of your parents," Patricia said, stinging from the things that he had said. Perhaps if she had felt less for him, they would not have had the same impact, but he had hurt her deeply and she spoke with less consideration of the effect of her words than she would do usually. "That is one area where you are most certainly like your mother. You are both handsome and have poor reputations, so you are the same in that regard."

The moment she said the words, she knew she had erred. Enid raised her eyebrows, clearly astounded, but Samuel's reaction was more marked. His posture stiffened, and he looked at her in surprise, but she could detect the hurt in his eyes.

Removing her hand from his arm, he bowed to her, his posture rigid. "I find it disheartening that after all that we have shared, you can still believe me to be a rake without conscience, as long as I am happy. That has never been who I am, and I thought you knew that. Apparently not. At this point, I would argue that you are showing more similarities to my mother than I. Please excuse me, ladies."

As he walked away from them, Enid turned to Patricia. "There is something havey-cavey going on here. I have my suspicions but am not ready to say my piece just yet. I will say that you need to decide what you want and show it, or you are in danger of losing everything."

Patricia watched Enid as she disappeared. She was mortified. Lashing out had never been her style, she was not that kind of person, yet she had uttered the words which would hurt the most. Just because he had unknowingly upset her, that did not mean that she had the right to hurt him. It had been a horrible thing to do, for knowing him well meant that she knew exactly how to strike to have the greatest effect.

Her cheeks burned with remorse. She had to make things right between them, but her thoughts were interrupted by Sophia. "Is everything well?" her friend asked.

"Yes," Patricia answered, her tone saying otherwise.

"You were all smiles when you came in, and after speaking with the earl's mother, you no longer show any hint of happiness."

Sophia's words did bring a lightness to Patricia's expression. "She has some odd notions. I do not think I will ever be overly fond of her." It was a convenient excuse to use Imogen as the problem.

"She does seem a little strange, but you can forget her now as she is seated far away from you. As always, it looks like it is going to be an enjoyable evening. Your grandmother certainly knows how to put on a dinner."

Sophia was right. The people who had been invited were those who would make conversing over a long supper entertaining rather than a trial. Added to the fact that Enid always put on a feast, being of the opinion that if food was left at the end, it was a fair indication that the guests were full. It was another sure way of knowing that everyone would be leaving with good memories of an enjoyable evening.

The only blot on the evening for Patricia was that Samuel had not looked in her direction since he had left her. He scowled when approaching the table, seeing they would be sitting opposite each other. It was not *de rigueur* to speak across a table, but they would be in sight of each other the whole evening, which was clearly something he did not relish.

Patricia's heart sank. Now she would not be able to clear the air but would see just how out of sorts he was. As she was the one who always tried to bring a smile to his face, seeing him so upset—with her as the cause—did not bode well for a pleasant evening.

Unusual for a seating plan, she was placed next to Juliet on one side and Frederick on the other. It was etiquette for her to be sat between two gentlemen, but it was a decision Enid had made to allow the two women time together. Patricia had to console herself with the hope that she would get to know Juliet by the end of the evening. It was the only bright spot she could think of.

Frederick started off in his usual way, looking delighted that Samuel was within hearing range and sending many smug looks in his opponent's direction. "My dear cousin, I am convinced you become more beautiful every day that I see you."

"I think you suffer from over-exaggeration," Patricia said, her tone unwelcoming.

"I am soon going to run out of words to compliment you."

Noticing the sardonic rise of Samuel's eyebrows, Patricia bristled, despite feeling terrible for hurting him. His reaction just confirmed to her how little he thought of her, reinforcing the words he had said to his mother—that he considered her the next thing to a pauper, and one who was not particularly comely, at that. "I find there are sometimes too many words uttered which should never have been, for they can hurt as much as a physical blow."

Frederick turned to her, lowering his voice. "I hope you have been able to understand my actions, my sweet cousin. I am ready whenever you give me the signal. I am eager to show you what I am prepared to do to make sure you are forever happy and content."

"Please stop. I am an engaged woman and I do not wish there to be a scene between you and my betrothed when this dinner is for welcoming Miss Barbosa."

"I just wish you to know that I am waiting."

"I am afraid you will be disappointed." Patricia hated the fact that she was feeling so uncomfortable. She had never wanted her cousin's attention and though it had stung when Samuel had ridiculed him for fawning over her, she had to agree that his actions were inappropriate. She turned away from Frederick, glad that he seemed to take the hint, for the moment at least.

"It seems you have two lovers to choose from," Juliet interrupted.

"You are very lucky."

"I think not," Patricia said quickly.

"There is no need to be embarrassed about being popular. To know you are a desirable woman is good for the soul. There is no better way to keep a husband in love by your side and at your beck and call."

Patricia snorted. "I doubt that very much."

"But yes!" Juliet exclaimed. "A lover who knows there is competition for his chosen one will work harder to make sure he is the best he can be for her."

"I certainly would spend my life making sure my cousin is cosseted and cherished as she deserves to be," Frederick said, blatantly ignoring the snort from Samuel.

Patricia refused to look in Samuel's direction. "Thank you, cousin. That is a sweet thing to say, but I as I said, I am engaged."

"For now," Frederick muttered.

"See, you have a choice." Juliet waved her hands. "They are both handsome, but their characters are night and day. I think you should have both! Then you would have everything." She laughed at Patricia's shocked expression. "You are disgusted with me."

"No, I am surprised, that is all."

"I have sailed the world and seen many things. I am not so easily shocked anymore. I know it is hard to believe, but I too was once as innocent as you."

"Does it have anything to do with innocence to want faithfulness and a steady character in the person you are to spend the rest of your life with?" Patricia refused to let the worldly-wise woman make her feel inferior when her views were so against all that Patricia believed in. This was as bad as her conversation with Samuel's mother. But it was also concerning that a woman her brother had fallen in love with might not be as committed to him as he was to her.

"If he is special enough, maybe." Juliet shrugged.

The way her words were delivered did not provide any reassurance for Patricia, so she decided to change the subject, hoping to find out more about the woman. "It is a pity your father was not here for tonight's gathering. We would all like to meet him."

"He would not attend even if he was in port," Juliet said. "He knows he would be out of place, so never ventures into society unless, of course, he needs to sell and barter his cargo. Then he will talk to everyone and anyone."

"He never escorts you?"

"Why should he do that?"

"I just presumed, with you having no companion, that he was the one who normally accompanied you."

Juliet laughed. "This is not good. I have shocked you again. I am no green girl, and no one would win if they tried to attack or proposition me. My father does not accompany me, but he trained me to fight, and I am never alone, nor unprotected, when I have a knife."

"You carry a knife?" Patricia had to stop her mouth from falling open with shock. "Here? Now?"

"But of course. Bad men are not confined to the London streets, or no naïve miss would ever be compromised. That is not something I would let happen. My looks can attract those whom I do not care for. I need to give them a message they will not misunderstand or forget."

"I suppose so. It just seems a little extreme."

"There will be men in this room who have a weapon at their disposal. Why should I not be as prepared?"

Patricia glanced at the diners. It was a sobering thought that amongst them, there were some who would hurt them if they were pushed too far, or at least, they had the ability to do so. Feeling like the innocent Juliet had accused her of being, Patricia took a large sip of wine, thankful that her grandmother did not serve lemonade to the ladies as some households did.

"Cousin, I would like to assure you that I carry no such weapon, and any gentleman worth his salt would not bring a weapon into the drawing room of such an esteemed person as your grandmother," Frederick said when Juliet's attention was diverted by the gentleman on her other side.

"I am glad to hear it. For the first time in a long time, I feel a little out of my depth," Patricia said. Taking another gulp of wine, she glanced at Samuel, who was having a long conversation with the girl on his left, though his dinner partner seemed a little overwhelmed by his attention.

Patricia felt a pang. Was it envy or panic? She could not tell. Nor could she berate them for their conversation. She had been the one to suggest he should be sat next to Miss Bertram. It looked as if her matchmaking skills were not needed after all, which just made her feel worse. And it had nothing to do with the bet they had.

She was so used to him sending her an occasional glance or pointed look when they overheard something funny or outrageous that now that it was missing, she felt bereft. Her spirits lowered further when she thought he would never look at her again with that smile which had been reserved just for her. It would be saved for when he met the woman he would marry. She knew him well enough to know that he would be a faithful husband and a doting one, and could only repine that it would not be her.

"The lady is too rough for my tastes, too uncouth, but I think your brother is pleased with her," Frederick said, interrupting her thoughts and bringing her attention back to him.

"I am sure it is just the way she has been raised that makes her stand out more than a newcomer would normally, although, with her good looks, I believe she would always attract attention. Her upbringing has been about as far away as possible from what is considered normal; it is no wonder she has different opinions," Patricia said quietly. "She seems to like Dominic a lot, which I can only be pleased about." She couldn't help wondering about how true Juliet would be to Dominic from what she had hinted at, but as they had not even announced an engagement, it was too early to be overly concerned about something that might or might not happen.

The ladies withdrew to the drawing room, and Patricia sat herself next to Isabelle and Sophia. She was glad to be away from Samuel— and Frederick for that matter. He was pleasant enough, but his flowery language and overly cheerful persona were draining after a time. That she had been sitting with him for hours had ensured that she left the dining table with a pounding headache.

"Is there to be dancing when the gentlemen arrive?" Isabelle asked.

"Grandmamma has had the card tables set up in the morning room. I think there will be too few to dance when the card tables are full."

"That is a pity, for I was hoping to avoid needing to perform." Isabelle grimaced.

"As the person with the most wonderful voice I have ever heard, I had already suggested to Grandmamma that you should be the first to sing."

"I thought you were my friend," Isabelle groaned.

"I am, which is why I need to promote you at every opportunity."

The gentlemen walked in, and Patricia could not help glancing at Samuel. But instead of seeking her out, as he usually did, he immediately approached Miss Bertram and sat next to her with one of his rare smiles. Patricia felt the twist of her insides at the action but had to force herself to look away. That Miss Bertram did not look to be welcoming towards Samuel was irrelevant; Patricia knew what a catch he was, and Miss Bertram's parents would certainly be overjoyed at the attention their daughter was receiving from him.

"Have you had a disagreement?" Isabelle asked quietly. She'd watched the scene play out and had obviously sensed her friend's discomfort.

"Not really. Oh, blast it, why am I pretending otherwise? Yes, we have. I said something to upset him, and though it was unintentional, it has caused him real distress. So, because of my stupidity and callousness, I cannot be angry that he wishes to be far away from me," Patricia said.

"To be flirting with another is not good *ton* and not very gentlemanlike. I am surprised he is acting in such a way. It is sure to cause gossip and speculation," Isabelle said.

"No. I suppose he should not be seeming to enjoy himself with another quite so much, but it is my fault and mine alone." Patricia could not reveal her earlier plan to find him a wife. It now made her feel physically sick every time she thought of it. "I must go and serve the tea. Excuse me," she said as the tea trays were carried in.

Distracted for ten minutes, Patricia looked up when Samuel got up from the sofa. She had sensed him the moment he had moved, though she had purposely never glanced in his direction. Still, there had always been an awareness between them. She had considered it was just because they were such good friends, but now, she accepted it was probably because she had been in love with him for a long time and had not acknowledged it.

Heart rate increasing as he approached her, she knew she had to make amends, but from the expression on his face, it was not going to be easy. Trying to calm her nerves, she had to at least make the attempt, for she could not stand the thought of him thinking ill of her. She would have to learn to accept that he felt no affection for her, but to lose his good opinion was too much for her to bear.

"Miss Bertram would like some tea, please." His tone was abrupt.

"Certainly," Patricia responded. "Would it be possible to have a quiet word with you at some point this evening?" Her hands shook slightly as she handed him the cup.

"I do not see any reason why that is necessary. I have spoken to Dominic; he is to stand guard tonight. Tomorrow I will speak to the relevant person to inform them that the Thursby's ball will be the last evening we will be performing our farce. I will return to my estate after that. I have suggested to Dominic that he might wish to remove you from town for a while in case the thief tries to strike after I have gone."

"Oh." Patricia was glad he had waited until everyone else had been given refreshments; at least they had a little privacy. She felt sick to her stomach at his words.

"I am sure you will be as delighted as I that this case can be brought to an end. I can only wish I had never embarked on such a foolhardy scheme. I suppose that the only advantage is that I now know your true opinion of me."

"You must not think that!" Patricia whispered urgently. "You are mistaken, I assure you."

"The evidence would suggest otherwise. Your words were quite clear—I did not mishear what you said. For me, there is nothing else to be achieved by further discussion." Samuel turned on his heel, obviously eager to be away.

"Samuel, what about the engagement?" Patricia asked, her mind racing to try and find a way to delay him.

"What about it?" He did not turn back fully towards her.

"What do I do?"

"Call it off after the Thursby's ball. I can retire to my estate in order to nurse my broken heart."

His words were said with such derision that tears flooded her eyes, and she left the room, hoping no one had seen her. If she had thought seeing him with another woman would hurt, it was nothing to how she felt knowing that she had lost his good opinion forever.

She had no idea how she would carry on without him in her life.

Chapter Nine

H E WAS IN a bad mood. In fact, he was in the foulest temper he
had ever experienced in his life. As his carriage trundled
towards Bow Street, he cursed and muttered the whole way. Blast her
to the devil! He was the one who had been wronged. The words she
had uttered had been downright offensive, so unlike her that it had
shocked him even more. Yet he had been the one to suffer a night of
tossing and turning, unable to get her tear-filled eyes out of his mind.

Why had he thought a pretend engagement was a good idea? He
should have listened to Dominic, but oh no, of course he knew better.
And it did not matter how much he tried to excuse his actions, he had
taken advantage of a friendship and it had blown up in his face.

The thing he would miss most was being able to touch her, watching how her eyes lit up when she spotted him and how his heart felt
light whenever he was around her. How she could make him laugh
with one look and tease him out of the worst of his megrims. Why did
she have such power over him? He now considered it was his
foolishness that had seen the interactions between them as meaning
more than they clearly did. To her, at least.

He had thought he was in love with her—no, he knew he was in
love with her. It had happened so gradually that he had not noticed
what strong feelings were developing until those feelings were so
strong, they frightened him. From the moment this scheme had
started, he had acknowledged that there was only her for him. He

could not have imagined anyone else working by his side.

He had hoped she was with him, but what she had said put paid to any notions he might have carried in his breast. He would probably spend years trying to convince himself that he had not really been in love with her. It angered him further to know the pain was not going to go away anytime soon.

When she had disparaged his character, it had felt like a slap. He had overreacted, but her words had caused a pain that would not have occurred if someone else had uttered them. Had she always thought so little of him? Part of him thought not, but it was easy to succumb to his insecurities. Especially when he did not know whether she felt as he did. Having never expected to feel so deeply for someone, he was at a loss as to how to deal with the uncertainty. Therefore, it was easier to think the worst in an effort to try and protect himself. If he managed to dampen down his feelings for her, he would not risk getting hurt. A pity it was probably already too late.

Unable to ponder further as the carriage arrived at Bow Street, his mood deteriorated further when he realised the court was in session and he would have to wait amongst the chaos which was Mr. Read's office if he wanted to see him that day. He took a seat with a deep sigh; being alone with his thoughts would not improve his mood in the slightest.

"This is an unexpected surprise," James Read said as he entered his office over an hour later.

"There is too much crime in this city," Samuel snapped, disgruntled at waiting for so long.

James laughed and, opening a drawer in a large cabinet that showed many signs of wear and tear, he lifted out a decanter and two glasses. "While there is poverty, there will always be crime. As long as people are driven by greed, I will forever be busy."

"Does the brandy help?"

"I allow myself a glass after court. It helps to clear the distaste from my mouth."

"Distaste? I could understand if you said the smell." Samuel accepted the offered glass and took a sip. It was surprisingly good brandy. On another day, Samuel would have teased James about the source of the spirit, but he was in no mood for funning.

James sat in his seat and took a gulp before leaning back, his eyes closing briefly as he enjoyed the feel, warmth, and taste of the brandy. "If I drank as much as I would need to forget the side of life I see every day in this god-forsaken place, I would be a roaring drunk within a week. The distaste is caused because I am issuing sentences which will send whole families into worse situations than they were in—situations which forced them to commit the crime in the first place."

"Anyone would think you do not believe in punishing them."

"Oh, I do. But I object to sentencing a woman who stole a loaf of bread because her children were starving, and she could not bear to watch them suffering any longer. Her husband had an accident at work, and his employer said it was his fault and turned him off. Now the mother has been convicted, the father still cannot work, and I have all but condemned those poor starving children to death."

"What about help from the parish coffers?"

"The same parish which looks upon any theft, whatever the motivation, as beyond redemption? The parish that considers not working a sin, though the poor man can barely walk by all accounts? The family was turned down for help, and as a result, she stole the bread. She had never stolen anything in her life before, so of course she bungled it and got caught. I have no problem sending the ones who deserve it to the gallows or transporting them, but I hate being the one to sound the death knell to a whole family."

Samuel was silent for a while, frown firmly in place. "Do you have their address?" he eventually asked.

"Why? Are you going to help them? You will soon come to the depressing conclusion that you cannot help them all. Believe me, I have tried."

"I accept I cannot do that, but I can do something for this family. I presume you did not send the mother to the gallows?"

"She is considering herself lucky as she got off lightly with six months in Newgate. It almost made me laugh when my clerk said that I was going soft. Anyway, enough of this. To what do I owe the pleasure?"

Samuel brought him up to date with what had happened—or had not, in this case. He didn't mention the argument with Patricia. "I am to return to my estate this week, so I need to bring it to a close. I will make it known that I will be leaving town the day after the Thursby's ball, and Dominic is going to take his family away to make it appear that we are leaving together."

"And the engagement? There has been a lot of speculation about it," James said with a smile.

"Miss Leaver will call it off when she sees fit," Samuel said coolly.

"I really thought our thief would have made a move by now. It is very disappointing, leaving us with very little to go on."

"It appears the thief is far cleverer than we first thought."

"I have known he is an expert. After the first theft, I was like you in that I thought this person was trying to make an insurance claim, especially with no sign of entry or exit. But then the second one happened, and then the third, and it was too much of a coincidence. As well, not all would wish to admit to the losses, nor need the insurance money. Is there anyone you think is suspicious enough to investigate further?" James asked without much hope.

Samuel pondered. "You will probably think I am a loose fish when I tell you about the two people who do not feel right to me, but they are the only two who I think could, at a stretch, be involved."

"I am all ears," James said, grabbing a piece of paper to make notes.

"The first is a nodcock." Samuel smiled at the look of derision

James shot in his direction. "If it is him, he is most certainly cleverer than he looks. His name is Frederick Heller and claims to be from Amsterdam. He introduced himself to Mrs. Leaver, saying he was some distant cousin. She says she remembers someone moving abroad when she was younger, but it all seems a little too hazy and convenient for me."

"Interesting. And he has only been around these last few weeks? The thefts have been going on for longer than that."

"It is a few weeks since he introduced himself. I have no idea who he knows and where he was before then. He is certainly trying to make an impression on Miss Leaver."

Samuel could only imagine what Patricia would say if she ever found out he had put Frederick's name down as a possible suspect. In the past, he would have enjoyed her railing against him, but after recent events, that easy relationship had probably gone forever. The thought completely depressed him.

"Who is the second one?" James asked. "More hopeful than the first, I hope."

"Er...it is a woman." Samuel raised his hands, a laugh on his lips. "She is out of the ordinary, and you said yourself that it could be a female."

"I did." James did not look convinced, but he waited for Samuel to continue.

"I do not say this lightly because Dominic is smitten with her, but it is Miss Juliet Barbosa. Her father owns many ships, and they travel all over the world, though they are originally from Portugal. I did not really consider her when I first met her, but the more I listened to her, the more I perceived how hard she is."

"Hard?"

"If I were to read the words she utters, I would think she was a man, if that makes sense? I suppose if she has been raised on ships, surrounded by sailors, it could explain some of her ways, but there is something about her which does not seem right."

"I can have them both checked out. With her father owning ships, she should be the easiest to trace. It would make the job of getting rid of the jewels almost effortless if they were constantly leaving these shores," James mused. "Though that isn't the best news for the women missing their finery, if there is no way to return them to their owners."

"I am sure they will survive the deprivation. Most will have had insurance."

"But not all."

"Then they only have themselves to blame." Samuel shrugged. "Do you have the address we spoke of? I would like to set something in place before I leave town."

"I will send it through to you. My clerk has the files from this morning. I will ask him to dig it out. It is a good thing you are doing."

"It is the right thing. Do not go trying to convince yourself that I am some sort of kind benefactor. I am not. But like you, I hate the thought of an injustice being done, especially to people with few options."

"Whatever the motivation, I thank you. If nothing else, this will help me sleep better tonight."

"I would not have your job for a King's ransom," Samuel said, standing and putting on his hat and gloves.

"Too few men and too many crimes," James said, also standing and shaking Samuel's hand.

"Oh, that reminds me. Dominic Leaver has expressed an interest in assisting, if you are willing to meet him."

"Is he reliable?"

"Yes, and loyal to a fault. He would be an asset, and on the small chance his chosen one turns out to be our thief, he will need a distraction."

James cracked out a laugh. "You are a cold one sometimes."

Samuel shrugged. "You make that sound as if it is a bad thing. My experience would suggest that it is anything but."

PATRICIA PREPARED FOR the ball with a sense of dread. They had all made it known that they would be leaving town soon after returning from the Thursby's estate. She had hated lying to her grandmother but had been forced to say that they would be staying at Samuel's estate and not going into what was effectively hiding. Dominic had been reluctant to tell Juliet a lie, but Patricia had warned him not to take her into his confidence. He was reconciled with the fact that he would return to London once Patricia was settled and safe. Juliet accompanied them to the Thursby's, which pleased Dominic further.

Patricia would have to confess everything to Enid before they left London, but she refused to dwell on the fact that she had spoiled her friendship with Samuel and was going to disappoint her grandmother in admitting that they had lied to everyone. She doubted that her grandmother would be sorry that she was not going to marry Samuel after all. Only she would struggle with that. In truth, the thought of not seeing Samuel for a long time was far more upsetting to her than anything her grandmother would say.

She still needed to make things right between them, or at least try. Trying to convince him that she was genuinely sorry had to be her main motivation for the evening. He might never forgive her words, but he had to know that she did not mean what she had said, that she had reacted out of spite because of his words to his mother. She had a sliver of hope that eventually he would forgive her if she managed to explain herself, but it was tiny. He could easily dismiss her actions as a sign of her true character, though she hoped he knew her well enough to know that her criticism was so out of character, she had shocked herself.

She fought to regain her focus as they trundled through the streets in the carriage. She could not let Enid suspect that something was wrong. Fortunately, Dominic was overflowing with chatter which filled the silence.

Walking into the grand home of the Thursby's, she pasted a smile on her face, ready to meet the hosts and pretend that all was well. She could not do anything about the fact that she knew her smile did not reach her eyes; she could not achieve the impossible. She was allocated a small room with an anteroom for a maid. Samuel had asked that she did not bring her own maid, which would enable her to sleep on the truckle bed while Samuel stayed in the main room.

It was a heck of a risk for her to take, but at the end of the day, they were officially engaged. It would mean that they would be forced into marrying if they were discovered, which, although she would be with Samuel forever, would be a miserable pairing, for him at least. And she would take no enjoyment from him being forced to marry her. She wanted him but would never stoop to compelling him into marriage; that would be as bad as his mistress claiming to be increasing.

Her troubled thoughts lasted all afternoon, but she tried to shake them off as she was helped by one of the Thursby's maids to dress for the evening. Satisfied that she looked the part of a newly betrothed woman, even if she did not feel it, she joined her grandmother, and together they entered the large ballroom.

The Thursbys might not be titled, but they were a very rich family and well-respected. The room was already bursting with people, and there were others still arriving. The chamber was decorated with foliage rather than flowers, ensuring there was a pleasant fragrance in the air, but it was not overwhelming. A trio of musicians were already playing a minuet, and a few people were dancing, but most were greeting friends and acquaintances before the evening's dancing started in earnest.

Relieved when she saw her friends, she abandoned her grandmother and made her way to them. At least seeing them made her smile genuine.

"You look stunning," Amelia said.

"Thank you." She had chosen a cream dress with a silver net overlay. The bottom edge of the skirt had two rows of delicate red roses, her whole outfit planned to set off the necklace around her throat to its best advantage.

"You have been avoiding us," Sophia complained. "We have not seen you since your grandmother's party."

"She is newly engaged. She does not want our company," Amelia teased, but Patricia had seen the look her friend had shot her. There would be no avoiding Amelia's questions at some point.

As they chattered, she scanned the room for Samuel, and her heart sank when she saw him near the Bertram family. He was standing a little away from them, and she could not, in all honesty, say that he looked happy, nor did Miss Bertram. But he was close enough to appear to be a part of their party. Patricia wondered if she was hoping that Miss Bertram looked uncomfortable rather than the way she actually felt. She did not know her, after all, just that she seemed pleasant enough.

Her parents must think it a strange situation, with Samuel engaged to another, but showing their daughter attention. It might be confusing for them, but watching it was torture for Patricia, and it had nothing to do with the speculative gossip Samuel's actions would be causing.

"I told you it would be hard to see him with someone else," Amelia said quietly. "Are you going to do something to bring him back to you?"

"No," Patricia said firmly. "I have hurt him, and it is better for him if he finds someone who can make him happy."

"His eyes are saying that he is very unhappy. I would say he is polite but indifferent to Miss Bertram. But there is pained longing in his expression when he looks at you," Amelia said.

"You are a hopeless romantic. Ah, cousin, you are here," Patricia said, turning to Frederick.

"I would not miss an evening spent in your company for anything," he gushed. "I realise your betrothed will be dancing the first with you, but could I have the second?"

"Of course," Patricia said, not knowing if Samuel would approach her for a dance or not.

"Then my enjoyment for the evening is secured." Amelia turned to answer a question from Isabelle, and Frederick took the opportunity to take one of Patricia's hands in his own. "Cousin, you must allow me to speak to you," he said urgently. "That man does not deserve you. I can see you are out of sorts, and I am going mad with the need to make you happy."

"Please, you must not speak this way," Patricia appealed, trying to unobtrusively pull her hand from his grasp, but he held fast.

"You cannot be still engaged to him! He has been chasing another woman, insulting you by even looking at someone else, let alone actively pursuing them. They are clearly smitten with each other."

"Are they?" Patricia felt sick and trapped in the last place she wanted to be. Her own confused feelings led her to give Frederick's comment more credence than she would have done in other circumstances. Why had she agreed to come to this event? She wanted to rip the damned necklace off and run until she could go no further. But her cousin seemed oblivious to her pain.

"Yes! He is a disgrace to all men and mostly to you. No one should betray someone as special as you are, my dear cousin."

"I am the one at fault," Patricia said, choking with emotion.

"No, you can never be so!"

"I am. He is not to blame. It is I who is a disgrace."

"Our dance is starting," Samuel said from behind Patricia.

Swinging round, she flushed, not knowing what he had heard. "You wish to dance with me?"

"Of course, we are betrothed, are we not?"

Holding out his hand, she automatically put hers in his. If she was shaking a little, she could only hope that he did not notice.

They stood opposite each other in the line. Patricia longed for the music to start, for only when they were close in the dance could she try to put things right. She had presumed he would remain away from her, and she was not about to waste this opportunity. If nothing else, she would beg his pardon. When the music started and she moved towards Samuel, she felt daunted at his impassive expression. She knew how well he could conceal his emotions, but not knowing what he was feeling was a new and unwelcome experience.

"I am sorry," she blurted out as she moved under his arm.

"For speaking what you truly feel? There is no need to atone if you were speaking the truth."

"No! That was not why I said what I did. I do not even believe in the words that I spoke."

"You do not usually utter falsehoods. You are one of the few people I know who says what she thinks." Samuel was angry with himself that his heart had soared at her words, but then he recollected himself. They had stung like no others. "I would suggest that it was something I needed to hear, for it is clear I have been offering friendship, unaware that you had such a low opinion of me."

Patricia could have cursed like any man did when they were separated in the dance but spoke the moment they came together once more. "I consider you the best of men and one of the closest friends I have."

"In that case, I am thankful I am not your enemy," he said bitterly. Why did he hate that she looked so upset? He was a fool and he had to remember what her words had done to him.

"You are not going to forgive me, are you?" Her voice was despondent, shoulders slumped.

"For voicing what I have heard time and again over the years by those in society who make it their business to give their opinions, no matter how ill-informed they are? No," came the cold reply.

The dance seemed to take an eternity; she had never felt so uncomfortable near Samuel in all the years she had known him. He was being belligerent, but she could hardly blame him. When the music eventually ended, Frederick's arrival prevented any further conversation, even if Patricia had had the heart for it. She went through the motions with the second dance until the woman in a couple who crossed them in the dance exclaimed as she reached for Frederick's hands.

"Mr. Wakefield!"

Frederick ignored the woman, but Patricia looked at him in surprise, the woman's exclamation pulling her out of her thoughts.

"Mr. Wakefield, do you not remember me? I was in Brighton with you last year. There was an almighty argument when you left, I can tell you. I cannot wait to tell you about it. I am sure you will be eager to hear what happened."

The dance pushed the couple onto the next pair as they moved down the line, but Patricia was watching Frederick closely. "Mr. Wakefield?" she asked.

"She is mistaken." Frederick shrugged, but his usual joviality was gone.

"She seemed very sure that she was addressing the right person."

"It is not me who she knows. Perhaps she needs glasses."

Patricia laughed at the remark, more for the way he expected her to accept such an outrageous statement. She was convinced the woman believed Frederick to be her Mr. Wakefield.

When the dance ended, Frederick almost dragged Patricia in the opposite direction from the woman who had moved down the line. "I think we need some refreshments, cousin," he said, guiding her to one of the refreshment rooms. When he grabbed a glass of punch and swallowed it in one go, Patricia thought it wise to put some distance between them.

"What is going on, cousin? You say that woman is mistaken, but she has rattled you. I would appreciate it if you told me the truth of the matter."

Frederick looked resigned and almost ready to speak but then cursed under his breath when the woman entered the refreshment room with another, clearly looking for him.

"Here he is! I told you it was him, did I not, Mabel? Who could forget those beautiful eyes or that charming smile?"

As there was absolutely no sign of a smile, Patricia could not help being amused, though she was watching her cousin closely. When it looked like Frederick was not going to speak, Patricia took over, needing to find out more.

"Ladies, please forgive me. My cousin seems a little surprised to see you, so allow me to introduce myself. I am Patricia Leaver."

"Pleased to meet you. It is no wonder he is shocked to see us after what happened in Brighton, is it not, Mabel?" Before her friend had time to answer, the first woman turned to Patricia. "Miss Leaver, I am Miss Brocket, and this is Miss Cherry. Your cousin was one of our party last year at Brighton."

"You never mentioned you were in Brighton. And last year? When here I was presuming you were much farther away," Patricia said archly to a fulminating Frederick. "It seems you managed to get up to some mischief. Ladies, you must tell me what happened."

"No!" Frederick said, finally finding his voice. "There is nothing to talk about. It was a visit to the seaside, that is all."

Both women giggled. "Oh, Mr. Wakefield, you are a tease. Brighton life was far duller when you had gone. If Cecilia knew you were in London, she would be here in a heartbeat," Miss Brocket said. "She swears that if she ever finds you, she will abandon her family, fortune and all."

Frederick paled at her words but said nothing.

"Your friend sounds like she was smitten by my cousin," Patricia continued to probe.

"Oh, she was. We had never seen two people so much in love, had we, Mabel? And just when everything was settled and arranged between them for the most romantic elopement ever, Cecilia's guardian returned to Brighton."

"How inconvenient," Patricia responded, a flicker of a glance at Frederick.

"Exactly! We tried to help by making a hasty escape with Cecilia, but we had hardly left the town when we were discovered. We were sent away in the most brutal, rude manner, her guardian threatening all sorts of nasty things if we ever got in touch with Cecilia, did he not, Mabel?"

"It is a shame that you lost a friendship over it."

"Oh, we didn't," Miss Brocket responded cheerfully. "One of Cecilia's maids gets to the post before the butler does. Cecilia writes to us daily, and I can honestly say that she is as much in love with you as she ever was, Mr. Wakefield. She will be over the moon to know where you are. It would not surprise me if she left the moment she receives our letter."

"She should not leave her family," Frederick said.

"Especially without her fortune," Patricia said with mock innocence.

"She does not care about that. She just wants to be with you," Miss Brocket said with a heartfelt sigh.

"Forgive me for the interruption, ladies," Samuel said from behind Patricia, startling her for the second time that evening. "I need to have an urgent word with Miss Leaver's cousin."

Noticing that he had not used Frederick's supposed name or the name the ladies knew him by, Patricia presumed he had heard much of the conversation. Feeling a twinge of disappointment that she had not sensed his approach, she looked at him with curiosity.

Samuel glanced at her. "You do not need to worry. I will sort this out."

"I am not worried, but I am coming with you. I also have something I wish to speak about."

The two ladies looked between Samuel and Patricia. "Is anything amiss?" Miss Brocket asked. "We can vouch that Mr. Wakefield is a perfect gentleman. It is not his fault that his family has fallen on hard times."

"It certainly is not," Patricia said, stifling a smile when Frederick closed his eyes in either exasperation or defeat, she was not sure which.

"Do not be alarmed. It is about his family that I wish to speak to him," Samuel said smoothly. "I am sure after our little chat, he will seek you out and help you to send the missive to your friend, saying that he is ready to marry her even without her fortune."

Patricia followed Samuel as they moved from the refreshment room, skirting the edge of the ballroom and out into the hall, Samuel surreptitiously holding onto Frederick's arm. The hallway was quite busy, but Samuel indicated to a footman to approach them, whispered something to him and with a nod, the servant led them to the library.

"I thought it best to ask for the library, thinking you would find comfort being surrounded by fairy stories," Samuel said grimly after he had tipped the footman and closed the door, locking it and putting the key in his waistcoat pocket. "Now talk."

Chapter Ten

S AMUEL WAS FURIOUS. He had never wanted to take a swing at someone as much as he did at this moment. He was livid, and it had nothing to do with the fact that Frederick had clearly been trying to secure the fortune of a young woman, though that confirmed just what type of man he was.

"Speak!" Samuel demanded. "And I want the truth. No more of your flummery nonsense. I have heard enough of that to last me a lifetime, probably two."

Frederick glared at him but then turned to Patricia. "You should not be here."

"I most definitely should," she responded. "I need to hear just how foolish my family and I have been in believing your falsehoods."

Frederick slumped onto one of the two chairs near the unlit fireplace. Patricia stood behind the opposite chair, gripping the top, while Samuel stood guard over Frederick.

"You had better start talking, or I will not be responsible for my actions," Samuel said.

"Fine! But I meant no harm," Frederick started.

"I will be the judge of that," Samuel replied.

"I am not a rich man. I needed a rich wife, but it is hard to find a woman who is perfect and not surrounded by family."

"The type of family who would quickly identify you as a fortune hunter and send you on your way," Samuel said with derision.

"Do not look down at me when you have no idea of what it is to live in this half-life!" Frederick snapped. "Born into the gentry, but not having the means to live the life that is expected."

"You could always earn your living," Patricia said quietly.

"And be ridiculed for that? No thank you. It seemed easier to find a rich wife."

"But her guardian appeared to have perfect timing," Samuel said.

"Didn't he just?" Frederick said bitterly. "He would not listen to Cecilia though she swore our love was genuine."

"Yet it was not reciprocated enough that you would marry her without funds. Her friends might not have noticed your reaction when you thought she would cast off her family and inheritance, but I certainly did," Samuel said.

Frederick glared at Samuel. "I can barely support myself; we would be in the suds if I had to provide for another. I think my reluctance shows sensibility rather than a lack of feeling."

Samuel did not believe his motivations for a moment, but he could imagine the girl's family would be relieved that Frederick seemed keen to distance himself from her.

"What is your real name, and where do you come from?" Patricia asked.

"Frederick Wakefield and I live in Scarborough."

"We are no relation, are we?"

"No."

"Why us? We are not wealthy," Patricia asked.

Frederick shrugged. "I overheard a conversation."

Samuel could see that Patricia was struggling with what she was hearing, and though he wanted to protect her from the upset, he knew she would not thank him if he tried to make her leave. The irony was not lost on him that not long ago, he had acted in a way he had known would hurt her, yet here he was, hating the fact that she was being upset by another.

"The conversation you heard must have been wrong," Patricia said. "We are comfortable, but from the way you were trying to convince me to abandon my engagement..." She shot Samuel an embarrassed glance, the first time she had looked at him since they had entered the room. "You clearly thought that my dowry was larger than it actually is."

"Then you do not know what is coming to you," Frederick said. "The conversation I overheard was between your grandmother and your brother. She said it had been a generous gesture on his part to forgo his part of her inheritance to ensure you had a comfortable life after she was gone but that you would not need it if you married *him*."

Patricia moved to slump in the chair she had been holding on to for support. She was pale and shaking. "I had no idea," she eventually said. "Dominic should never have agreed to it. Whatever Grandmamma leaves us should be split equally. Just because I am not married to a rich man does not mean my claim on her funds is any greater than Dominic's."

"He was being a good brother," Samuel said. "Knowing him, it is of no real surprise."

"Yes, you know us both well enough to know what we would do in any given situation."

"I thought I did."

"I am truly sorry."

"As am I." His fists were balled at the urge to go over to her, which annoyed him, but he always felt the need to make things right for her. He did not seem to be able to change, though he had tried. "They should have told you because it could have made a difference to what decisions you made."

"I was determined not to marry, until I met you," she said quickly remembering to maintain the farce. "But that does not mean I was relying on Dominic not receiving what was his due. I would rather be set to work doing needlework."

Her words made him smile, in what seemed like the first time in a long time. He knew her upset was on Dominic's behalf and not on her own account; she always put others first.

"You would starve if you had to rely on your needlework earnings."

"Brute, though I cannot argue against you."

"That is a first."

"I have come to the painful knowledge that I am far from perfect and need to not believe all what is said."

Samuel frowned at her. There was clear meaning behind her words but he had no idea what she was referring to.

"This is all very sweet, listening to you both, but I would like to return to the party if you have finished with me," Frederick said.

Glowering at him, Samuel was annoyed that he had been more concerned in finding out what had gone wrong between himself and Patricia than concentrating on the task at hand. He would need further conversation with Patricia, but for now, he had to remain focused in order to find out if Frederick had anything to do with the thefts.

"You clearly decided that Miss Leaver's future wealth was enough of a draw that you concocted this Banbury tale of being a long-lost cousin."

"I could not believe my good fortune when your grandmother said there had been a family member who moved abroad. It was music to my ears," Frederick said.

"But I was engaged!" Patricia exclaimed.

"Yes, that was a little inconvenient, but I had also heard your grandmother quizzing your brother about what the reality of your match was. From the discomfort on your brother's face, I knew there was something amiss, so decided to try my luck. You have to admit, we would make a fine pair, and we get on perfectly." Frederick looked confidently at Patricia.

"Do I have to admit such a thing? I think our views differ greatly on the matter," she responded. "I seem to remember constantly telling you that you were being inappropriate and to stop spouting flowery speeches."

"Inappropriate?" Samuel almost snarled, looming over Frederick, who shrank in his seat.

"Not in any way which you need to concern yourself about," Patricia quickly interjected.

Samuel tried to collect himself, but it was not easy. The rage he had felt at the thought of Patricia being at the mercy of a cad like Frederick was almost overwhelming. He had never felt such absolute anger towards another person as he did towards this man who had tried to trick Patricia into marrying him just so he could access her fortune. He was not sure how James would react if he received the potential jewel thief beaten to a pulp, but he felt that it was an inevitable conclusion at this point. Still, something about Frederick made Samuel doubt he was the thief they were seeking. He had to find out for certain though. It was unlikely Frederick would mention Samuel's line of questioning to anyone else. Especially if Samuel made sure he left town right away.

"While you could not access Patricia's funds immediately, you decided that jewel theft was a profitable use of your time," Samuel said.

"What? Jewel thefts? What are you talking about?" Frederick spluttered, sitting up in his chair, panicked at the accusation.

"There have been some items of value taken from the homes of the wealthy in recent months. The suspicion is that it is someone on the inside of society who can come and go without raising suspicion and, if the help of servants is required, can charm them to do their bidding. You have openly said that you are charming, though personally, I cannot see it."

"Good God! You are accusing me of this? You must be out of your mind!"

"Not at all," Samuel said, tone calmer. "You have only appeared in our midst these last few months, just when the thefts started. You have charmed your way around society, and you need funds. Tell me, how are you getting rid of them?"

Frederick jumped to his feet, terror on his face. "It is not me, I tell you! I would not have the wherewithal to do something like that."

"Yet you have changed names at least once, created a new identity and wormed your way into the lives of people who did not know of your existence. You are clearly a very accomplished liar," Samuel pointed out.

"I have done nothing more than try and secure an advantageous marriage!" Frederick insisted. "I fully admit that, but I have stolen nothing. I will not swing for a crime I have absolutely no knowledge of."

"Why should we believe you? Do you think we are fools enough to accept this new set of lies?" Samuel taunted.

"I am not lying! Not this time anyway." Frederick sat back down. "Good God, I could hang, and I have done nothing wrong."

"I doubt the family of Miss Cecilia would agree to your view."

Frederick scowled at Samuel. "You know full well what I mean. Just to be clear, I would have cared for Cecilia as she deserved if we had married. I needed money, but I am not heartless." He turned to Patricia. "I would have cared for you too. I am not an unfeeling brute like the one you have aligned yourself with. How can someone so vibrant attach yourself to him? I have seen his eyes—cold and detached—as they scan a ballroom. You deserve so much better."

Frederick was snatched out of the chair by Samuel. "You think you deserve her? You would never be worthy of her," he snarled.

"What I find insulting on Miss Leaver's behalf is that you consider yourself good enough. It would be funny if it was not so offensive to her. She would wilt in a marriage to you; you drain the pleasure wherever you go."

"Damn you!"

Samuel's fist connected with Frederick's jaw with a sickening thud, sending him sprawling on the floor. Samuel towered over his prone body, ready to continue as soon as Frederick moved.

"You can do what you want to me, but it does not make my words any less truthful."

"You would not know the truth if it slapped you in the face," Samuel snarled, fists clenched.

"I know it would be very convenient for you if I was out of the picture, but believe me when I say you may be the lord, but I am no thief, and I refuse to stand by quietly whilst you try to get me out of the way by sending me to the gallows. Just because I do not have the funds I would like, that does not mean that I would resort to theft."

"And you expect me to believe that?" Samuel almost laughed.

"Enough." Patricia had stood and placed her hand on Samuel's arm. "We have heard all that we need to. He is not the thief you are looking for. You know it as well as I—he never did quite fit into what had been going on. There is absolutely no point in continuing this. It achieves nothing which can help."

Her voice was a mixture of resignation and sadness, and it pierced Samuel's heart. He stepped back from Frederick, glancing at Patricia's pale face and hating the scoundrel even more for causing her distress.

"He is a cad and a fortune hunter, who is going to leave London today," Patricia said, looking at Frederick as she spoke. "We will never see him again, but the thefts will continue. I do not think he has the capability or intelligence to undertake them."

Frederick stood but glared at Patricia. "There is no need to be quite so disdainful. I spoke well about you."

"As she has quite likely just saved your life, I would watch your tone if I were you," Samuel said. Patricia's words had broken through his rage. When slightly calmer, he agreed with her assessment of the situation. "You are nought but a pretty face and a fawning nature. I am glad I will never have to see you again."

Frederick stood, rubbing his cheek, but he turned to Patricia as he moved toward the door. "I would have done everything in my power to make you happy. And though it risks another punch, I stand by what I said. You deserve better than him."

"Yes, she does," Samuel said, unlocking the door. "Now get out of my sight."

The door closed as Frederick cut his losses and made his escape before Samuel had time to change his mind. They were left staring at the closed door, both reluctant to break the silence in case the hostilities between them resumed.

"We are no further on with this blasted crime," Samuel said.

"I suppose we know of one person who is not guilty," Patricia responded.

"I am sorry," Samuel said eventually, turning to Patricia, full of remorse.

Patricia had been through a myriad of emotions during the exchange with Frederick, but it was nothing to the surprise she felt at Samuel's words. "Why are you sorry?"

"That his falsehoods have hurt you. But if it is some consolation, I think he genuinely cared for you." Samuel did not quite meet her eyes as he spoke, fidgeting and seeming unsettled.

"Why would that matter?" Gripping the back of the chair again, she waited for him to speak.

He sighed. "I know you cared for him. I did not want you to feel that his actions were purely mercenary. I could tell he spoke the truth when he said he valued you."

"You are mistaken. I did not care for him at all."

Samuel smiled gently at her, at last meeting her gaze. "You do not need to be brave with me. I know you."

"Clearly not very well if you thought I would fall for his flowery nonsense. I was polite to him because I thought we were related. I am not sorry that he is gone from our lives. In fact, I am quite relieved. I am just upset that we cannot issue some kind of warning to prevent him from fooling anyone else. Men like him tend not to give up easily."

Samuel sighed as if a weight had been lifted from his shoulders at her words. "I am glad that you have not been hurt. I wanted to kill him when I thought you had feelings for him and he had abused them with his falsehoods."

"No, I did not and would never have been taken in by him." Patricia was torn. She wanted to throw herself at him, begging him not to marry Miss Bertram, but she could not. If he thought she was attached to Frederick, his own heart must have never been hers. "Tonight is to be your last night with us?" she asked.

"Yes."

"You will be glad to get a good night's sleep in your own bed."

"Yes."

Patricia could not help the smile that tugged at her lips, but she soon became serious. "I am truly sorry that I upset you. I have no excuses to offer, but I reacted badly to what you said to your mother and I am so very ashamed that I acted in such a poor way. It was badly done on my part."

"What I said to my mother? What did I say that upset you so much?"

"About marriage not being all about good looks and money."

Samuel paused, frown in place. "But surely you do not think it should be about that?"

"Well, no, but it is hard to hear, even when it is your fake betrothed, that he does not consider you eligible in any regard."

"But I was not referring to you." Samuel was utterly confused.

"Of course you were."

"No. I was not. I was trying to make a point to my mother. She was considered pretty and had a good dowry and look at the marriage she had. I would never have spoken in such a way as that about you."

"I do know my own limitations; I just think hearing the words on your lips surprised me. I felt as if I had been struck. And so, I hurt you."

"I thought your opinion of me was something you had hidden but that it matched the rest of society."

Taking a step towards him, she hesitated and stopped before reaching out to him. "I think very highly of you—perhaps a little too high if I am being honest. Since my stupid words were uttered, it has been the worst of times. I have hated that we have not been as we normally are with each other. I have constantly wanted to beg your forgiveness until I convinced you that I was in earnest, but at the same time, I understand why you withdrew from me. It was that knowledge which should have stopped the words from being uttered in the first place, but I was being addle-pated and cannot excuse it."

The hopeful look in Samuel's eyes made her feel like the worst kind of fool. He was a man who spent so much of his time separate from everyone else, and his isolation had always been of concern to her, for she knew whatever façade he put forth, he must be lonely on so many occasions. It made her ache for him even more.

"Is there such a thing as too high a regard?" The words were said with a little of his usual swagger or an attempt at it, at least.

"You brute." She tentatively smiled at him. "You know full well how highly I think of you, have always thought of you."

"For the first time, I doubted it, doubted you."

"I know, and I will be forever sorry about that. What we have shared over the years, how you have been with me, I have always treasured and could not believe how bereft I was when I lost your good opinion. I hated this time of being apart from you."

"You will have to work out a way to show me just how wonderful I am," Samuel teased, at last looking at her as he usually did.

It was an expression Patricia had never seen him use with anyone else, and finally she at least could breathe easier that their friendship had not been completely destroyed. As for anything else, well, that was going to be over in the morning.

"As the one who is to break my heart tomorrow and force me to cancel our engagement, I would say that I need to choose my future beau with more care. I doubt there will be any more fortune hunters, especially when I have spoken to Grandmamma and insisted that she changes her will." She was trying to match his funning tone, to make their separation easy, but to her own ears, her voice just sounded strained.

"You are not returning to life as it was before our engagement?"

"Being a confirmed spinster and accepting my fate?" Patricia smiled. "No. This experience has taught me that it is good to spend time with someone you know is always looking out for you. A person you can talk everything over with no matter how silly. The one you seek out the moment you enter a room."

"I have always looked out for you," Samuel said gently.

"I know you have, and I have been grateful for it, but this false engagement has given me a little taste of what life could be like with the right person." Patricia was revealing too much to him. She was trying to explain, badly, how he made her feel and why she would try to understand when he married someone else. She would force herself to be his friend. "Miss Bertram is going to miss you when you leave town."

"Who? Oh, I do not see why." Samuel looked nonplussed at the change of topic.

Patricia chuckled. "You have been spending a lot of time with her."

"I thought that was what you wanted me to do. I presumed that was part of the plan, to give everyone the message that the engagement was not a happy one."

"No! I did arrange for you to be sat next to Miss Bertram, but—"

"And seated yourself next to that blaggard, across from me, giving me a clear signal of your intent, or so I thought."

"No, that was not of my doing."

"I doubt anyone will expect anything to develop between Miss Bertram and I when you call the engagement off. She squeaks in fright whenever I speak to her. It is quite off-putting and not very flattering."

"You can be rather fearsome when you want to be."

"I was trying to be nice because I thought it was what you wanted."

"That was the last thing I wanted. Oh! Why are we even having this conversation? My friends say that you look at me differently than you do anyone else, but I know it is only because we have been friends for so long."

"I do not wish to be your friend," Samuel said, moving from behind the chair which he had been using as a protective barrier, frightened to reveal what he was feeling, to be so vulnerable in front of her. But it was now the moment to act, or there would always be barriers in his life. It was time to take a risk with the only person he had ever wanted to be with.

"Oh, I am sorry to hear that. That thought makes me so desperately sad." Patricia could not stop the sudden rush of tears which immediately spilled down her cheeks unchecked.

"Please do not cry. I hate to see you upset. I always have. It is like a stab to my stomach whenever you are unhappy, especially when it is I who has caused it. Patricia, I should never have taken umbrage at your words. I think it was just my insecurities that had me acting so over the top. I never realised that my own words could have been misconstrued," Samuel said. Pausing, he ran a hand through his hair, still uncertain. The confidence he exuded in society completely deserted him in a moment which could destroy him if it went wrong. "I have never done anything like this before. I do not know how to go about it without making a hash of it."

"Done what? I have no idea what you mean."

"Been engaged to a woman first and then asked her to marry me," Samuel blurted out in what was probably the most unromantic speech ever uttered.

Patricia stared at him, open-mouthed. This was what she had wanted. But she had barely allowed herself to hope that he would speak to her at the beginning of the evening, so this was a heady turn of events, even for her. "Marry you? Are you being serious? Are you sure that is what you want?"

"Never more so. Do I need to worry that you consider I might be funning with you over such a matter?" His tone was light, but there was a vulnerability about him that Patricia had never seen before.

"It is just unexpected. I can hardly comprehend the change that has occurred," she said, feeling a little breathless, thoughts crashing one after the other.

"Is it such a surprise? Have I not always sought you out, offering the real me, the only one of two people who have ever seen that side of me."

"I have always loved our bond."

"As have I. Now I am asking for more. If you will allow me, I want to be the one you seek out in any room you are in, the one who is the first to greet you in a morning and the last to kiss you goodnight at the end of the day. I did not understand just how much I loved you until I thought I had lost you. I am not sure how coveted the situation is, but you are the only woman who has made me feel jealousy, desperation and happiness."

"That does not sound like a pleasant situation to be in."

"I think the only way to overcome it is for you to be by my side for the rest of our days. Will you marry me, Patricia? For I have only ever given one person my heart, and that is you."

"You are in earnest," Patricia almost whispered. "I can hardly believe it. I truly did not know you felt so strongly. I knew you held me in affection—I just presumed it had always been as a friend."

"I cannot tell you when it changed. It was before this case, but it was in trying to find the thief which brought home what I feel. And though part of me is terrified, I know I will only be happy with you."

"No one can be happy always. I hope you do not have such unrealistic expectations."

"Does that mean I am to be rejected?" Samuel asked, taking a step away from her, his expression changing to one he would always fall back on when in company. It revealed nothing of his inner thoughts and was off-putting to anyone foolish enough to wish to engage him in conversation.

"No!" Patricia almost shouted, and then laughing at her outburst, she took hold of his hands and pulled him towards her. "No, you could never receive a rejection from me. I have been in love with you for I have no idea how long. But when I stupidly pushed you towards someone else, I did it purely because I thought you felt nothing for me in return."

"I feel pleasure, pain, love, frustration and amusement, amongst other things where you are concerned." He smiled at her. "Never accuse me of a lack of feeling."

Patricia reached up to him and touched his hair, sliding her hand to his cheek and cupping his face, loving the feel of his skin, the slight stubble which covered his lower cheek, though he would have shaved before the ball. "You are very good at flowery speeches when you want to be. It is something I have not noticed before. Have you been taking lessons from Frederick?"

Pulling her into his arms with a growl, Samuel kissed her. It was a kiss built of anxiety, longing and love. It was no gentle, tentative kiss—this was the action of a man proving himself to the woman he loved, and though inexperienced, she relished the way he teased her lips until she opened them for him and allowed him to explore her mouth, her jaw, her neck, as if he had been starved too long.

Wrapping her arms around his neck and pulling on his hair, she felt as if she could not get close enough. Her body felt alive in a way that sent tingles through her and a sense of excitement and longing that she had never felt before. When she pressed herself against him, and heard his moan of pleasure, she felt powerful, pleased at the effect she had on him as their bodies seemed to fuse in harmony with each other.

"It has been torture having you so close and not being able to touch you," he whispered between kisses. "I have hated these last days. I was a fool."

"I felt so lost. I missed you coming to the guest chamber to wake me each morning, I loved how you stroked my hair, and touched my shoulder. I did not want you to leave."

"Neither did I, but it is a good thing that I did not know your feelings then, or the maids would have had a shock. And your grandmother would have punished me for the rest of my days."

Patricia chuckled. "It certainly would have caused a fuss. Can I at least be woken by a kiss or two in the morning? A real kiss, not your usual peck."

Samuel rolled his eyes. "Are you trying to torture me?"

"Probably." Patricia grinned. She was almost drunk with happiness and relief. She had gone from utter despair to absolute joy in one evening and never wanted it to stop. She had a future with the man she loved, and nothing else mattered. He loved her.

"I never want you to stop tormenting me," he said, kissing her some more.

Patricia pulled away suddenly. "But you are leaving London, and so are we!"

"I will speak to Dominic," he said. "You can all come to my estate. I would rather have you close, and we can plan a real wedding this time. Do you think it could be arranged within the month?"

"That would be nice," she murmured. "Are you really giving up on this case after tonight? I am surprised that you are not keen to find out who the culprit is." It was time to be practical, though she just wished they could continue the kisses and forget the rest of the world for now.

"Yes." Samuel struggled to gather his thoughts. "There is no firm evidence to suggest who it might be. I have given Mr. Read some potential leads, but as one was Frederick, I do not think they will come to much. I was keen to solve it because of the standing it would give me, the approval of royalty showing that I am worthy to be in society. But I have come to the conclusion that I only need you by my side in order to have everything I need."

"Oh Samuel, I wish that you were not affected so much by what others say about you. You are so much better thought of than you think."

"Only because I have a title and money. Not because of who I am."

"Then we should continue to solve this, for no other reason than to prove that we make an excellent team."

"I am more than ready to give it up. I am not made to stay awake all night."

"This from Bawdyhouse Bentham? I am shocked!" Patricia laughed as he kissed her once more.

"Fine, we will carry on with the usual plans for tonight. I could not have guessed that I would have a potential Bow Street officer in my wife."

"Stop your flummery. I am still offended that you would even consider a member of my family a criminal, but I can understand why you did."

"Let us not forget he is of no relation."

"Thankfully. Does this mean we can take a ride in your curricle before we leave town tomorrow, and actually behave like a real couple for once?"

"I have considered us truly engaged since the start. It was a surprise when my feelings came to the fore, and in many ways was an unwelcome turn of events," Samuel said. He was still holding her, unable to let her go now she had admitted her feelings for him.

"Why?"

"Because I was going to suffer when it was broken off as we had agreed. A man who has never been in love but then falls heavily is not going to recover quickly or easily. You know me well enough to understand that I do not do things by half. If I make a commitment, then I give it my all. That is why I decided to leave. I would not have been able to see you each day and not be a part of your life, not in the way I longed to be."

Patricia reached up and touched his face, gently stroking her fingers along his chiselled cheekbones. "We are a pair, are we not? This could have turned out very differently. I thought that was going to happen for certain, and I, too, did not know how I could bear to be near you, and not be with you. Now though, we are together, and I can look forward to showing the world that we are indeed in love."

"Let us start immediately." Samuel took hold of her hand as they moved to the door. "Oh blast."

"What is it?" Patricia asked. She was not confident enough yet to believe fully that her road to happiness was going to be smooth.

"I have just remembered that I am making a visit tomorrow morning." Telling her the story of the family who were in dire straits, he finished with, "I could send a basket of food to them and be done with it. But I wanted to attend in person to see if there is any help they need which will improve their situation for longer than the food will last. Does that make sense?"

"It does and it is commendable." Patricia smiled at him. "You really are the best of men, and I am so happy that you are mine. Would you object if I accompanied you?"

"The area is going to be unpleasant and rough," Samuel said.

"I am no wilting wallflower. Well, I was a wallflower, but I have never been of the wilting type."

Samuel laughed. "No, you most certainly have not."

"I could rummage out some clothing and toys. I know Grand-mamma stores everything in the attics. They will not be fashionable, but the material could be used, or alterations could be made to make them usable."

"From what Read said, I think looking fashionable will be the least of their worries."

Patricia slapped her hands to her cheeks, looking mortified. "I have just become one of those ninnyhammers with no sense of reality. Of course, they will have no interest in fashion!"

Samuel kissed her nose. "You could never be so flighty. I under-stood what you were trying to say."

"Then you will indeed be a perfect husband if you accept my faults so easily. Come, there is dancing to enjoy with my betrothed."

Chapter Eleven

PATRICIA HAD NEVER felt so happy. The rest of the ball had gone by in a blur of teasing, dancing, and never being apart from Samuel. She had felt a pang of guilt when she saw the expression of surprise on Miss Bertram's face, but she also sensed a hint of relief in her look. Patricia would still regret having used Miss Bertram ill, but her remorse could not take away her feelings of pure joy knowing that Samuel loved her.

When she was undressed, she dismissed the maid sent to help her. She should go to the truckle bed and shut the door between them; they would be closer than they had ever been, and that thought alone had her heart racing. Instead of doing the sensible thing, she put on her dressing gown and waited nervously in the main chamber.

Samuel paused when he opened her chamber door. His eyes raked over her, darkening as he swallowed. Coming into the room and closing the door quietly, he remained standing near it, not moving any further towards her.

Suddenly feeling as if she had erred, she resisted the urge to run into the anteroom. "Hello," she said quietly, cheeks flushed with embarrassment and uncertainty.

"This is not a good idea," Samuel said gruffly, but he could not stop his eyes from roving over her body, making Patricia tingle as if he was touching her. She said that he had never glowered at her, but he had never looked at her in this way, either. There was such hunger in his expression, longing even, and the way he was breathing suggested his body did not agree with his words.

"I did not want the night to end. I have never been happier." She was suddenly shy and unsure if he would think less of her for being so forward.

At her unease, Samuel crossed the room in quick strides and took her in his arms. The awareness that he could not bear the thought of her being discomfited was both enlightening and unnerving. His happiness had never been so reliant on another being content. "Your words make my heart soar, for I assure you that I feel the same way. But it is not right for us to be together. Yet."

"I know I am acting like a doxy. You must think me awful."

He smiled at her, touching her hair tenderly. "As we are to marry in a few weeks, you most certainly are not. Believe me when I say that I will be the happiest of men if you greet me in this way at any other time. My resistance is purely because, on the small chance of the thief trying their luck tonight, I cannot risk being unable to react because we have enjoyed each other."

Patricia laughed, still deeply embarrassed. "Surely spending the night with me would not have such an effect?"

"Oh, my wonderful innocent. When we are able, I will enjoy showing you just how all coherent thought can disappear during a night of passion. And it will be a whole night, for I refuse to rush when the moment is right. We have both waited long enough, so I am set on ensuring we take our time."

The words made Patricia's heart race, and she felt such longing, her body ached. "In that case, I suppose we should wait."

"Yes, we should, but please believe me when I say that it is taking every ounce of willpower I possess to resist you. I have never wanted you more than I do now." He twirled a strand of her hair gently between his fingers.

Patricia did not want to leave but accepted what he said. "I was nervous about being intimate, but I long to be close to you though I do not understand most of what I feel," she said, never feeling so shy.

"There is no need to be afraid or unsure, for when the time is right, we will both enjoy each other. I will do everything in my power to make it immensely pleasurable."

"Goodnight, Samuel," she said, moving away from him, an unexpected warmth racing through her at his words.

"Good night," he replied hoarsely.

Closing the door on the anteroom, Patricia leaned against the smooth wood of the door, breathing heavily.

They were going to need as quick a marriage as she could arrange.

A NOISE DISTURBED Patricia from a deep sleep, and she immediately jumped out of the truckle bed, grabbing her dressing gown and flinging it around her shoulders as she ran out of the room and into the hallway.

Her official chamber door was open, and without hesitation, she ran towards it, bare feet not feeling the cold as her panic about Samuel's safety overtook all other considerations.

When she arrived, Dominic was only a step behind her. "I heard a shout," he said, immediately entering the chamber.

"Something woke me up, too," Patricia said. "Where is Samuel?"

There were clear signs of a struggle, and the box with the fake necklace in it had disappeared. Patricia looked around the room. Where was Samuel?

"Stay here," Dominic said, leaving the room.

"Not a chance," Patricia muttered, but she picked up the poker from beside the fireplace before leaving. She was not about to abandon Samuel, but she knew she was no fighter. The poker might just prove a useful weapon.

There was no sign of Dominic as she reached the stairs, and her bare feet made no sound as she carefully went down them. She was grateful no one else seemed to have been disturbed by whatever sound she and Dominic had heard. It would take some explaining if she was seen wandering the hallways at this time of night with only her nightclothes on.

Pausing when she heard another sound, she immediately went to the library. Dominic was at the open door leading out onto the terrace and Samuel stood near him, nursing his hand, which was wrapped in a handkerchief.

"You are hurt!" Patricia immediately dropped the poker with a clatter and ran to Samuel's side.

"I am sorry if I woke you and sorrier still that the blasted thief managed to get away."

"That does not matter," Patricia said. "Let me see."

There was a cut across his palm, but it did not look too deep. Samuel winced when she pressed the area around it while examining it.

"What happened?" Dominic asked, closing the door and pulling the shutters closed.

"I had dozed off," Samuel said with some shame. "I think knowing it was going to be the last night made me relax a little too much."

"I do not know how you have done it for so long," Dominic said.

"Still want to join Bow Street?"

"I admit it does not sound as appealing as it did at first." Dominic grinned at him. "Perhaps I am more inclined towards a pampered lifestyle than I first thought."

"Good!" Patricia said.

"I am not being serious."

"I wish you were. I will return shortly with something to clean and bind the wound." As she turned, she was startled to see the butler dressed and looking surprisingly alert.

"I can bring what you need, Miss Leaver," he said, as if it was perfectly normal to witness the scene before him. "Oh, and Mrs. Leaver would like to be informed as to what is going on." The butler left them to stare in horror at each other.

"Oh Lord!" Dominic said. "That is a conversation I think you should have with her, Patricia."

"But you are the head of the family, remember? I think it should be you who speaks to her."

"As the head of the family, I can command others to do my bidding," Dominic said airily.

"You are definitely not suited to Bow Street if you are afraid of your grandmother," Samuel chipped in.

"Is that right? Just wait until she hears you have been spending every night in Patricia's chamber. We will see then who is the coward amongst us," Dominic responded.

Samuel swallowed and looked at his friend, real consternation on his face. "I had not considered she might find that out."

Dominic grinned. "Not so brave now, are you?"

Patricia moved to the door, accepting the items she needed from the highly efficient butler. "Please tell Grandmamma that we will explain in the morning but for now, all is well."

"Certainly, miss. Is there anything else you need from me?"

"No. You can return to bed. Thank you for your assistance."

The butler inclined his head and left the group alone once more, closing the door to the library.

Patricia turned to Samuel and Dominic. "You two need to be serious while Samuel tells us what happened. We need to work out if there are any clues as to who the thief is."

While Patricia started to clean Samuel's hand, Dominic went to the side table and poured two glasses of brandy. Handing one to Samuel, he sat down near him.

"Did you get any indication of who he is?" he asked.

"No," Samuel said through gritted teeth. "I had the curtains closed around the bed except for the one facing the window. It meant that anyone entering the room would not catch sight of who was in the bed, but I still had a fast escape if needing to apprehend them. As I drifted off, the first sound I heard was when the jewellery box was moved."

Patricia finished her ministrations and, moving the bowl of water and cloths onto the desk, she sat next to Samuel. The need to be close to him was almost overwhelming. She felt as if she moved away, he would be in danger again. It was a ridiculous thought but not one she could easily release.

"I had clearly caught him by surprise, for he let out a yelp of shock when I jumped from the bed. But he was cloaked and dressed all in black. When he lunged at me with the knife, I just grabbed it instinctively. Not one of my best ideas." He smiled ruefully.

"You could have been seriously hurt," Patricia scolded gently.

"Better to grab it than wait for it to strike him," Dominic said in support of his friend.

"I managed to grab his hand and twist it. I think I might have broken something, the way he shouted out. It was almost a high-pitched scream, which was somewhat satisfying."

"That must have been the noise we heard," Patricia said.

"He then managed to pivot his body in a way that made me stumble, and he ran. He clearly knew the layout of the house, and I am presuming the windows were already open because he was gone when I reached the library. I ran outside, but he had disappeared, though I heard the sound of horse's hooves in the distance."

"If you have hurt him badly, that could lead us to learning who he is," Patricia said.

"Whoever is absent from the party or appears with their hand bound is our man," Dominic said. "It seems you might have achieved more than you first thought."

"I will send a note to Read. I must return home, for I need to make plans to track them down. I have the real necklace on me, so at some point I must return that. Can I rely on you to send an express the moment you realise who is missing or if someone has a visible injury?" Samuel asked Dominic. "I have a feeling they will not return here, but if someone is missing, their absence is almost an admission."

"I will."

"Please stay here," Patricia said quickly, not looking at her brother. "You could become ill."

Samuel smiled warmly at her. "It is a scratch, truly. If I go now, there will still be time to visit the family we have spoken about. Should I collect you at four? Will you have returned home by then?"

"We will stay for breakfast and hopefully see everyone before we leave," Dominic said. "Most will attend breakfast while the party is breaking up this morning, so it is a perfect opportunity to discover who attends and who does not."

"Then I shall see you later this afternoon. Try and get some sleep."

"What about you?"

"I will catch up at some point. I will bid you both goodnight," Samuel said, standing. He smiled softly at Patricia before leaving but did not attempt to kiss her.

Ignoring the narrow-eyed look Dominic aimed in her direction, she stood, trying to stifle a yawn. "It is time for bed. I will sleep in my own chamber. Now that the thief has the necklace, there is no need for caution."

"No, I suppose not," Dominic said, finishing his drink. "We will speak further after we have both had more sleep."

"If we must," Patricia said in response, sensing that the theft would not be the only topic of conversation.

WHEN SAMUEL ARRIVED at four, he entered the hallway at Patricia's home and paused, a shocked expression replacing the smile he had worn as he entered.

Patricia, her hands on her hips, grinned at him. "Do you think this is too much?"

Samuel raised his eyebrows. "A portmanteau? Is it full?"

"It might be."

Laughing, he shook his head. "I am glad we have the carriage and not my phaeton." He nodded to two footmen, and they carried the heavy box outside. "Come, my love, let us help this poor family."

When they entered the carriage, Samuel pulled Patricia onto his knee, gently tugging her bonnet free to kiss her. "I could not say goodbye as I wished last night, but I can say hello this morning," he said, kissing her again.

"What if people see us?" Patricia asked, the curtains on the carriage windows open.

"Then they will be jealous of me." Letting her know how he felt with his kisses made him feel less vulnerable, for Patricia responded in a way that set his pulse racing. They only separated when they were both breathless and Patricia's pupils were dilated, her gaze unfocused.

Patricia leaned into him, and he held her close, her head on his shoulder. They fit together perfectly. When she looked up at him, she received a quick peck on the lips as he smiled down at her.

"Now is the time to stop," Samuel said gently. "I would not take you last night, and I will not in a carriage either, though I might suffer as a result of restraining myself."

Swiping his shoulder, Patricia moved off his knee with an embarrassed laugh, trying to straighten her dress and grab her bonnet, which had fallen onto the floor.

"I need you to know that it is torture to see you so tousled, and more, to know that I have to be good."

Smiling at him, she shook her head. "The more you speak like that, the more I think we need to get a special dispensation to marry."

"Would you be willing to do that?"

Patricia could not help the surge of affection she felt at his eager expression. "I would be more than happy. A woman beyond her salad days cannot afford to hang around when she has such a desirable offer."

"Be serious. You are far younger than I." He scowled at her. "I thought it was every bride's dream to have a big wedding?"

Patricia sighed and looked out of the window for a few moments. She could feel Samuel's eyes on her, but she needed to gather her thoughts to express herself fully and without the risk of causing any distress to him. Finally looking at Samuel, she was warmed at only concern in his eyes.

Taking hold of her hands, he kissed them gently. "What is it?" he asked.

"I am very lucky. Please do not think I consider myself otherwise. I have the love and support of Grandmamma and Dominic, I have dear friends and now have you. Lots of people would say that I have everything."

"But you do not have your parents," he said, understanding instinctively what affected her.

"Yes. If I were to have a large wedding, I would miss their presence dearly. But if I have a small wedding, with those I love, I will not feel their absence quite so much."

"We can have whatever wedding you wish. I just want you to be happy."

"I am! I truly am. I just hope you understand what I mean. It is no reflection on you, your reputation or the gossip that has plagued you. I have the urge to shout from the rooftops that I am the one fortunate enough to have tamed Bawdyhouse Bentham, though I hope not too much because you have always been the man who is the most fun to be around."

Giving her a wry look, he seized her hands once more. "I really should not have revealed that name, should I?"

"Oh, I don't know. It made you even more appealing."

Samuel laughed. "You really are a minx. But there is no need to worry. I completely understand your meaning. I would much rather have my father there than my mother."

"You cannot say things like that!"

"I think I just did." He grinned at her. "On a serious note, how did you explain away what happened last night? Did your grandmother give you a grilling?"

"She tried, but we just played it as if I had been in the room and not you. We swapped our places, saying that you had heard a noise and had come running."

"Which I would have done, if I had indeed been in another room."

"Precisely."

"Did she believe you?"

"Probably not," Patricia answered. "I think she accepted it far too easily. But Dominic said not to look a gift horse in the mouth and to just feel fortunate that she was not grilling us further. I think further questioning will come, but I distracted her enough to stop talking about what had happened. Still, she said she was surprised that I was not more upset about losing the necklace."

"Ah, of course she would notice that," Samuel acknowledged.

"Dominic actually told her off at that point, saying that all that mattered was that I was well and alive. He added that you had been injured, and that fact seemed to do the trick."

"Dominic sent me a missive to say that no one was missing nor showing signs of injury."

"No."

"What is it?"

Patricia sighed. "I feel a brute saying this, but the two people who claimed to be indisposed this morning were Miss Barbosa and Miss Bertram."

Laughing and shaking his head, he kissed her hand. "You cannot be seriously considering that Miss Bertram was the thief?"

"I do not see why it is any different than Frederick. Women can be just as unscrupulous as men."

"That was completely different." Perceiving that jealousy fuelled her words, he took hold of her once more. "Are you upset that Miss Bertram might have been in the same chamber at the same time as I?"

"Oh, stop it!" she cursed him. "You know full well that I am going to be a little touchy where she is concerned."

"She could never compare to you." All laughter gone, Samuel looked at her seriously. "You will never have to worry about my loyalty to you."

"But what you said previously about being unable to commit…" Patricia paused as the carriage stopped, and they both looked out the windows, unable to continue their conversation.

"Our arrival is ill-timed, but we will continue this later. It is too important not to," Samuel said. "In the meantime, Read has sent a note around to the family, so they should be expecting us."

The arrival of a fine carriage in a part of London that clung to respectability with its fingertips had caused quite a stir. People came to their doors or stuck their heads out of windows while children whose clothing had seen better days swarmed around them.

As Samuel handed Patricia out of the carriage, she looked around, taking everything in. "You arranged to have a great number of footmen accompany us," she pointed out, only just noticing that there was a driver and four footmen.

"I was not taking any chance that you would be at risk from someone who might think it a good idea to relieve us of our purses," Samuel answered. "I have never been to this area before today but guessed at how it would be. I am not about to make any assumptions when your safety is concerned."

There seemed no threat, but they both knew that situation could change in an instant. Having armed footmen was a wise precaution.

"I will give you the signal when to bring everything else in," he said to the head footman, grabbing one of the baskets of food which had been inside the carriage with them. The man nodded and stood guard around the carriage along with the others.

When he knocked on the door, a young girl of about seven or eight answered, and she opened the door wide.

"Pa says please come in," she said formally as if she had been learning the words.

"Thank you," Patricia said, smiling in encouragement.

"Pa can't come to the door. He's hurt his back," the child explained.

Samuel and Patricia stepped into a single room. It was dark, with only one small window and the door letting in any light. They could see it was clean, but there was no fire in the hearth and no sign of any food. A curtain that would normally separate the one bed from the living area was pulled open, showing a thin, gaunt man lying on a piece of wood on top of the bed.

A listless two-year-old sat by him, and there was another child playing with matches in a game of pick-up sticks on the cold floor.

"Forgive me, my lord," the man said. "I might faint if I try to get up, and it frightens the children if I fall."

"Be at ease. We have come to offer help, not increase your problems," Samuel said.

The man frowned. "Begging your pardon, sir, but I don't understand why. We got the note from the magistrate, but I had not heard of you before then, and I'm sure you have never heard of us, though I mean no insult."

The was no trace of the lofty aristocrat when Samuel smiled at the man. To see him so at ease in these surroundings made Patricia love him even more. She was fully aware of how most people of their acquaintance would have reacted in this same situation.

"Your hesitance is completely understandable," Samuel said. "The magistrate was forced to act because of the crime your wife committed, but he understood the dire circumstances that had driven her to it."

"We have never done anything like it before nor since," the man said.

"I believe you."

"What have you been doing for food?" Patricia asked.

"One of the neighbours gave us a loaf of bread and another some vegetables for a stew. I can't risk the girls making the fire; the pots are too heavy for them."

"Well, Mr...." Patricia paused, waiting for him to answer.

"Albers, my lady, Peter Albers."

"Well, Mr. Albers, the pots might be too big for your lovely girls, but they are not too big for me," Patricia said, not correcting his assumption that she was Samuel's wife. "You are not in any hurry, are you, my dear?" she asked Samuel.

"It would appear not," Samuel said dryly.

Chapter Twelve

PATRICIA TOOK OUT an apron and, taking off her bonnet and spencer, set to work. "Please ask the footmen to bring everything in from the carriage," she instructed Samuel.

The footmen carried in all the baskets of food they'd brought, as well as the portmanteau. All the family looked stunned. Patricia could see the children were desperate to eat but were too shy to ask, and her heart melted that though they were near starvation, good manners prevented them from asking for something to eat.

"This food will take some time to prepare. Would anyone like some bread and jam to start with?" Patricia asked, laughing when she received squeals of excitement at her words.

She handed Samuel a bread knife, and he looked at her dryly. "Putting me to work too?"

"Most certainly. You cannot just sit there looking pretty."

The two older children giggled at Patricia's words, but Samuel simply grinned at them. "Miss Leaver thinks I am pretty. Do you think she is right?" The eldest child nodded shyly, and he waved the knife in her direction. "An extra thick slice for this young lady who has exquisite taste."

Patricia shook her head at him as she chopped vegetables and meat, throwing them into the large pot which had been hanging forlornly from a hook next to the hearth. One of the footmen had lit the fire while Patricia had been working. When she had finished and put the pot over the now established fire, she warmed some milk up and gave the children a cup.

"Come here, little one," she said, leaning to pick up the youngest from where she still sat next to Mr. Albers. "Let me make sure you drink this all up."

"This is all too much," Mr. Albers said with tears in his eyes.

"Nonsense," Patricia replied. "I am afraid the clothes in the portmanteau are old, but I am sure they can be made useful."

"Thank you, miss. It is very good of you to think of us."

"We need to talk practicalities," Samuel started, once more sitting down while the children demolished the thickly sliced bread. "You need a doctor, help around the house, and someone who can cook, clean and look after the children until your wife is released."

"That all takes money, and even if I could work, my wages wouldn't stretch that far. We are already behind with the rent."

The look of shame on his face stirred Patricia. It was wrong that a single event could make an honest family spiral into debt. "I can sort all that out," she said quickly.

"There is no need." Samuel smiled at her. "It is already in hand." Standing, he handed Mr. Albers a pouch heavy with coins. "This will be enough to straighten everything out, pay for a helper and buy food when what we have brought with us runs out."

"We don't deserve this," Mr. Albers said quietly.

"Nonsense, you have three beautiful children who deserve the best," Patricia said. Placing the baby near her father once more, she stood straight. "I think a good wash is in order, and then we can see if the stew is ready for eating."

Patricia busied herself with warming water and stripping the children down to try to get rid of some of the grime. The house might be clean, but without an active parent, it was clear that washing had not been a priority.

Whilst Patricia was busy, Samuel pulled his chair closer to the injured man. "Where did you work before your accident?"

"At the docks, sir."

"And a ship owner cast you off?"

"Not quite, sir. He's a captain, but he doesn't own the ship. He works for the East India Company, but the men hate it when the ship he is in docks."

"Why?"

"He rushes the loading and unloading. I'm not the only one who has been hurt because of it. Trouble is, he rages when something happens, blames it on us and demands that we be banished from the dock."

"And no one challenges him over it?"

"No sir. The company brings so much trade to the docks, no one would stand up to them, afraid they might take their trade elsewhere."

"I suppose it puts the master in charge in a difficult position," Samuel mused. "When you have seen a doctor and had a few weeks to recover, I will send my man of business to you. He can work out what you are able to do and find you suitable employment. He will also replenish the supplies we have brought today."

"Thank you," Mr. Albers said. "I know I keep saying it, but this means everything. I thought our children were going to die." The last words were said so the children would not overhear, but his voice cracked.

Samuel looked at the girls being scrubbed clean by Patricia. "They look like good girls—you should be proud of them. You have been dealt a hard blow, but it is done now."

"I will never forget this kindness."

Samuel looked a bit uncomfortable at the words but nodded in acceptance of the compliment. "One last thing," he said. "I want to make my own enquiries about this captain. Pacifying the company should not involve people being seriously injured because of one rotten apple. There might be something that can be done about him.

What is his name?"

"Captain Barbosa," Mr. Albers answered, not noticing the look that passed between Patricia and Samuel.

It was another hour before they left the house, leaving the family fed and cleaner than when they had arrived. Patricia and Samuel had both been hugged by the girls, making Patricia laugh and enfold them in an embrace. Samuel, on the other hand, had patted them on the head awkwardly and shot Patricia a look of appeal.

As the door of the carriage closed, Patricia turned to Samuel. "It is too much of a coincidence!" she said, having barely contained herself while in the house.

Samuel nodded. "Not quite how Miss Barbosa described herself."

"No." Patricia looked troubled. "I wonder what else she has misled us about?"

Samuel looked at her cautiously. He did not wish to return to any misunderstanding or estrangement between them, but he did not want to hold anything back from her, either. "I have thought there was something amiss with her for a while now."

"Have you? Oh, poor Dominic," she said. "He will be devastated; he thought she was the one he would marry. I did wonder at his sudden attachment and the fact she is so different to the type of wife I expected him to choose, but if she made him happy, that would have eased my worries."

"I thought you liked her."

"She makes me feel a green girl—she is so worldly-wise. But that was not what made me feel she was not quite the one for Dominic. She seemed quite hard, and I always thought he would attract a fun-loving wife, someone similar to his own character."

"Does that mean you are grumpy with a dislike of society?" Samuel asked archly.

"Brute!" Patricia laughed. "In some cases, it is best to marry someone who is like day to your night, to balance you out."

"Ah, that explains it."

"I can see I am to have my hands full," Patricia said airily.

"Luckily for you, I am the type of husband to dote on his wife."

"Good to know."

"I need to speak to Read before we say anything to your brother. The information needs to be checked before we voice any damning accusations. I know I would not appreciate being presented with suspicions rather than facts, especially in regard to the woman I love."

"Barbosa... It is such an unusual name," Patricia mused. "Wait a moment, why do you need to check with Mr. Read? What has Bow Street got to do with whether Miss Barbosa's father is purely an unscrupulous captain or if he has a fleet of ships?"

"I was hoping I would get away without explaining that," Samuel answered ruefully.

Crossing her arms, Patricia glowered at him. "You had better start speaking."

"You are magnificent when you are angry." He smiled at her, but she continued to look unamused, and he sighed. "I asked Read to check out Miss Barbosa, ahem, in addition to Mr. Heller," Samuel said with a cough.

"Tell me you are funning with me," Patricia demanded.

"Afraid not."

"Of all the sneaky, double-crossing, low things to do!" Patricia exclaimed before slumping in her seat. "But you were right about Frederick. He was a thief of sorts—just not the one we were looking for, so I cannot curse you to the devil too much."

Samuel burst into laughter, making Patricia smile. "Oh, do not ever change, Patricia. You are a delight."

"Does this mean we are going to visit Bow Street now?"

"No, we are not," Samuel said, all laughter gone. "I am returning you home, and then I will send a note to Read asking when I may attend."

"And you will not take me when you receive a reply, even though I am involved?" Patricia said.

"No. I was not at ease taking you this morning, and I am certainly not taking you to Bow Street. The nearby streets should not be seen by a lady."

"Are the people very wicked?" There was a gleam in Patricia's eyes.

"You are incorrigible! It is an experience you should not have, nor want to have, for that matter."

"I hope you will not be one of those husbands who will treat me as if I would faint if I witnessed anything slightly shocking."

"I would like to protect you from everything unpleasant, but I know you well enough that if I tried, I would come off the worse for it."

"You must surely be reassured after this morning? I was not perturbed in the slightest about the area or what we found. In fact, I thought I was extremely productive."

"You were," Samuel said with real admiration. "I was very impressed. I would have just delivered the goods, told him my man of business would be in touch and left, thinking I had done my bit."

"And those poor children would not have had a warm meal in their belly. Goodness knows how long it has been since they have eaten something wholesome," Patricia said, tsking.

"You can feel suitably smug that you knew exactly what to do and performed as if it was second nature."

Patricia looked at him loftily but then started to smile. "Should I tell you a secret?"

Samuel was amused at her eager expression. "Go on."

"As soon as we returned from the Thursby's house, I spent the morning with Cook and a kitchen maid who has many brothers and sisters. They told me exactly how to best help Mr. Albers's family. It was the first time I had chopped vegetables, and although Cook shook her head at my lack of proficiency, she said the poor family would be so desperate for nourishment that they would be grateful for even my attempts. I did tell her Rome was not built in a day, and she threatened to give me lessons every week if I continued with my cheek. I had a great time, and the poor kitchen maid nearly had apoplexy in trying to stop laughing."

Samuel growled, grabbing hold of her and pulling her onto his knee. "Here was I thinking you were absolutely amazing, and it was all an act."

"Oh, I can assure you that I have many amazing qualities."

"I am looking forward to discovering them all."

His words made Patricia breathless. They had gone from teasing to something far more serious. Samuel's eyes had darkened as he caught one of her curls, twirling it between his fingers. Every time he was close to her, he touched her hair as if he could not help himself. She wanted to be kissed by him but waited, watching what he would do.

Smiling at her, he stroked her cheek. "I want to forget everyone else for now and concentrate on enjoying you. Have you any objections to that, or does it make me an unfeeling brute who is able to cast off the concerns of those less fortunate?"

"As you have set in motion solutions to their problems, there are no objections whatsoever from me," Patricia said before being kissed in a way that assured her she was not the only amazing one in the carriage.

When Samuel helped Patricia out of the vehicle, she looked positively dishevelled, with flushed cheeks and hair coming out of its clips and peeking below her hurriedly pulled-on bonnet.

"Are you still leaving today?" she asked, seeming a little unsure now that they were out of their own private space.

"Not until we get to the bottom of who Miss Barbosa is and if she is in any way involved with the thefts."

"You are still considering her as a possibility?" Patricia asked. "The thief got away from you, and though Miss Barbosa is no wilting flower, she could hardly fight you off."

"If she did, l am using fatigue and the fact she had a knife as an excuse. Otherwise, I will never live it down."

Patricia smiled. "No, you most certainly will not." Then she frowned. "Wait… At the gathering Grandmamma held, Miss Barbosa told me she always carried a knife. So maybe, it could have been her, right?"

Shaking his head, he smiled. "She certainly needs to be considered. I will return this evening sometime, but I might be a few hours."

"Fine, but I want a full update when you come back. No more keeping your suspicions to yourself. We are in this together."

"I knew I should have proposed to Miss Bertram. She would have been a meek wife and have done my bidding without complaint."

Patricia was about to argue, but then she leaned closer to whisper in his ear. "I will bet she does not kiss as well as I, or look as good as I did in a nightgown."

Samuel groaned. "You really are going to be the death of me if we do not marry soon." He shook his head at her again. "Go inside, minx, before I grab you and show everyone that I am definitely besotted."

"You always have to best me, you brute," she said, blushing. "Goodbye, but hurry back to me."

"Always, my lady," Samuel said, walking her to the door and kissing her hand.

As soon as Patricia had entered the house, Samuel strode down the steps and nodded to his driver. "Bow Street."

He climbed into the carriage. Today was going to be far busier than he had expected, but it finally looked as if he was getting somewhere.

Chapter Thirteen

S ITTING IN JAMES'S office, Samuel told him what had happened with Frederick at the ball and then all about the interesting morning visit. "I did not really consider the smooth-talking coxcomb as the thief, but I knew something was not right about him," Samuel finished.

"And it had nothing to do with him chasing a certain young lady," James responded. "Oh, do not shoot daggers at me. I hear gossip too. I am not constantly confined to this building."

Samuel shrugged. "If you listen to tattle, you will never hear anything good."

James smiled. "Maybe not, but it is always interesting and usually very entertaining."

"Did you find anything out about Miss Barbosa?" Samuel changed the subject from himself, never quite at ease when he was the focus of attention.

"I confirmed what Albers told you. Some of it was on the court file from Mrs. Albers's statement, and I put the request out for further questions to be asked on the docks."

"Was there anything forthcoming?"

"Captain Barbosa is indeed her father and he has a terrible reputation. His own sailors hate him, by all accounts. He is brutal, cuts corners to make the most money and very often moors at other ports that are not on his schedule."

"Why does he do that, I wonder?"

"Indeed. It is likely they are getting rid of goods, but in a way the East India Company will not be aware of. His ship is the HCS *Fearless*."

"An apt name, if what we suspect is true."

"Most certainly. Colonel Bannerman is coming to visit me this evening. There are a few issues I wish to discuss with him. You are welcome to join me if you think he might have some insight into what is going on at the docks."

"No, thank you," Samuel said. "I want to take a look at the ship myself, to see if there is anyone sporting a hand injury which they would have received last night. Perhaps the captain is the one who carries out the robberies when his daughter has gathered enough information."

"Be careful. He sounds like a man with few morals and no conscience."

"I will not approach him, but I will be armed, just in case."

"If there is any sign of the thief, send a message, and I will send everyone I can spare to support you. If everything goes well, we could have this blasted case closed, and I can concentrate on the real crimes that are happening daily."

Samuel smiled. "You will not be disturbed in the slightest that the jewels are probably gone forever."

"Not at all. I am with you regarding that, but I would never admit it publicly, of course," James said with one of his amused looks.

"I will keep you informed." Samuel stood and left the room.

Reaching his carriage, he retrieved two small pistols and, secreting them in his pocket, he nodded to his footman. "I will take a hackney from here to the docks. You can return home. There is no need to tell anyone where I have gone, just that I have business to attend to."

"You are going to the docks alone, my lord?" the footman was betrayed into speaking in what could be considered out of turn.

"You think I am incapable of looking after myself?"

"No, my lord, I am s-sorry," the footman stammered.

"Be at ease, man. You are probably right. John, give him your greatcoat. I cannot have him in his uniform if I take him with me. We might as well shout our arrival if he is so conspicuous."

The footman took off his wig and frock coat, wrapping the driver's greatcoat over him. There was little he could do to hide his shoes, but as they would be in a hackney carriage, they would be hidden if he did not have to leave it.

"I hope you can run in those," Samuel said, pointing to the buckled shoes. "If we see anything of note, I will be sending you back here for more men."

"I can, my lord," the footman replied, looking delighted to be going on some sort of secret mission.

"Good. First thing is to go and secure a hackney," Samuel said. It was time to get to the bottom of what had been going on. He wanted to be able to focus on Patricia and arranging a wedding.

WITHIN AN HOUR of being stationed at the dockside in a carriage, Samuel's idea paid off. Sitting in the hackney within sight of the *Fearless*, both he and the footman had watched the comings and goings to the ship with interest.

"It looks about to set sail," Samuel mused. "Come on, Miss Barbosa, where are you? Are you not going to wish your father a safe journey? We need you to bring your father out to see if I can identify him as the person who attacked me. Because if you carry a knife on your person, it is likely that he does, too."

Only there had been no sign of the captain. It did not mean he was not on deck, just that he had not come within sight of their position.

As if he had conjured her, Juliet appeared, walking quickly along the dockside, cloak billowing out behind her, completely ignoring what was going on around her.

"Well, I'll be," Samuel said, not hiding his surprise. She was the thief, after all—the bandage on her wrist was plain to see. "I need to have a word with her before she gets on that ship. She must still have the necklace on her. If she has, the evidence will be irrefutable, and the case closed before the night ends."

"Should I take a message to Bow Street, my lord?" the footman asked.

"Not yet," Samuel answered, climbing out of the hackney. "Wait here. I do not wish to cause a scene if I can avoid it. I might be able to bring this to a close without any fuss." The fact that he should indeed be returning to Bow Street, Samuel pushed aside. He was annoyed that they had been taken in by Juliet, and his pride was dented by the proof that he had been unable to stop a mere woman during the theft. But he refused to acknowledge that it was his wounded pride urging him on.

Juliet continued to stride across the docks, looking perfectly at ease, though her presence caused some cat-calls from the sailors. Ignoring the taunts, she wove her way through the obstacles, unaware that she was being observed.

"Miss Barbosa," Samuel called out, moving quickly to intercept her.

There was a flicker of surprise in her expression when she saw who was approaching her before she schooled her features. "My lord," she said coolly. "What are you doing here?"

"I thought I would come and look at your father's ships, however many there are in port, obviously. Oh, do not be annoyed," he said, noticing her flash of anger. "When a friend is clearly besotted with you, it is prudent to find out a little more about the lady in question."

Folding her arms, she glanced at the ship briefly but said nothing. Turning her attention back to Samuel, she stared at him, remaining impassive until he smiled at her.

"Ah, so it is true that you have embellished your father's position a little, have you not? He is not quite the owner of a fleet of ships as you led us all to believe."

"Does it matter?" she snapped. "Dominic does not need to marry into great wealth, and I have money."

"He is no pauper, I grant you. But I think he would like to know the truth about the woman he cares for."

"Then I will tell him." She shrugged in her flamboyant way. "I have things to do. There is nothing more I have to say to you." She moved to step around him, but he put out his hand to stop her. She glanced once more at the ship, and Samuel followed her gaze. Their interaction was being watched by a scowling man who stood on the deck, arms folded.

"Ah, I see the family resemblance," Samuel drawled, raising his hat in greeting. "You are eager to get on board, yet the ship is clearly about to set sail. Are you leaving us, Miss Barbosa?"

"I am to say a farewell to my father. You are delaying me."

"I am sorry about that, but I am afraid that I need to delay you a little longer. I am sure your father will not mind. I find it extremely coincidental that we are each sporting an injury—a new injury—which neither of us had yesterday." Samuel took off his glove to show his bound hand. Juliet was not wearing gloves; her bandage was too bulky for the delicate material to cover. "I would not be at all surprised to find out that you carry about you the necklace worn by Miss Leaver last night. Perhaps you picked it up by mistake? If so, I would be happy to return it to its rightful owner."

"Get out of my way!" she snapped, once more trying to step around him.

"No. I think today you will not be waving your father off, if that is indeed what you were intent on doing. I have the suspicion that you were about to leave these shores. After all, explaining a wound could be a little difficult when you went to bed unharmed and woke up injured."

Juliet glared daggers at Samuel. "You are interfering with matters that do not concern you. It will be the worse for you if you do not walk away now and forget you ever saw me."

"As much as I would like you to be far away from my friend—for I am of the opinion he would never be happy with you as his life partner—we need to go somewhere more formal and talk about this attraction to jewels you have. Some would say your dark locks remind them of a raven. Personally, however, I would say you are like a magpie, stealing shiny things from others."

"And you think you can stop me? That I will come with you and confess all?" She laughed at him. "You, who could not stop me in the dead of night? If I could beat you alone, you have no chance of besting me when I have a ship full of men who will do my bidding."

"They would attack a member of the aristocracy? Who would risk swinging for that?"

"Me," a voice said behind him.

Before Samuel could react, something hard hit him on the side of his head, and the world went black.

THE FOOTMAN JUMPED out of the hackney, demanding the driver wait for him. Running towards Samuel, he was roughly pulled back by numerous men. Starting to fight against their hold, he received a punch to his jaw, which made him stumble against two of the men who held him up. The one who had delivered the blow looked at him with some sympathy.

"Are you trying to get yourself killed, boy?"

"They have my master!" he appealed to them.

"That may be so, but as a toff, he has a chance at remaining alive. You, on the other hand, are dispensable."

"But they are carrying him on board!" The footman watched as Samuel was half-carried, half-dragged up the gangplank, clearly unconscious.

"Can you swim?"

Surprised at the question, the footman shook his head. "No."

"Neither could many of the sailors who did something to annoy the captain. Don't suffer the same fate. I'm sorry for punching you, lad, but it really was for your own good."

The footman sagged once more against the men who were holding him up. "I cannot just leave him to their mercy."

"If your master has friends, I suggest you alert them and tell them not to come unarmed. That captain isn't one to give up his captive easily."

"But if they sail before I can return?"

"Then they are sailing for China, so you will have a long journey ahead if you wish to follow them."

Running back to the hackney, he almost screamed. "Bow Street, as fast as you can!"

The men watched as the hackney charged away from the docks. "You should have told him his master is all but lost to him," one of the workers said to the man who had done the talking.

"I didn't want him throwing his life away on trying to save someone who is already beyond saving."

"I can't believe Barbosa is into kidnapping the gentry now. That is a sure way to end your days swinging at the end of a rope."

"I would not be shocked at anything that man does. I just wish someone was capable enough to bring him down," the first man said. "Looks like they are wasting no time in departing now they have him on board."

"They know if they are caught, there won't be an escape for the lot of them. The toffs don't like their own being hurt."

"Aye, no one cares about us lot, but when one of them is hurt, all hell will break loose."

"Best make ourselves scarce then before his friends start looking for him and asking why we did not help. They won't understand that we value our lives even if they don't."

"Yes, head down and mouth shut, then we live to see another day. Poor man won't be seeing these shores again."

They looked over to the *Fearless* one last time before returning to their duties. A man had to look after himself, after all.

Chapter Fourteen

P
ATRICIA WAS WALKING downstairs when a commotion started at the front door. Passing under the archway which led to the square entrance hall, she saw the butler arguing with a frantic young man.

"What is it, Jones?" she asked.

Before the butler had time to answer, the visitor spotted her. "Miss Leaver, I need to speak to Mr. Leaver urgently. They wouldn't listen to me at Bow Street, and they've got the earl!"

Palpitations thundered in her chest, but she reacted immediately, maintaining her calm, outwardly at least. "Jones, get my brother now and send him to the library. Do not underestimate the urgency of my request. He needs to attend immediately. Please follow me—"

"Terrence, Miss Leaver."

Patricia nodded. "Of course, Terrence, please follow me." If her hands were shaking, she gripped them tightly to hide the fact. If there was a problem, if Samuel was in trouble, acting like the wilting, weeping type of female she had claimed not to be would not help him. She had to remain strong and in control, for now at least.

Dominic entered the library only minutes after Terrence had arrived. "Patricia, what is going on? Jones is not happy," he said. His eye narrowed, taking in her stricken expression. "What is amiss?"

"Tell him," Patricia instructed, sinking into a chair.

"It's the earl, sir. When he dropped Miss Leaver off, he visited Bow

155

Street and then sent his carriage home whilst we took a hackney to the docks."

"He promised he would not do anything so foolish!" Patricia cursed.

"Why was he going to the docks?" Dominic asked.

"He knew who the thief was, or he suspected it. Turns out he was right. But he jumped out and challenged her. Then one of the sailors attacked him, and they dragged him aboard ship. I tried to reach him, but I was stopped by three men. They were dock workers, and they said people disappeared overboard when they upset the captain of that particular ship. They told me the best thing I could do to aid the master was to get help."

"So, you came here?"

"No sir, I went to Bow Street, but the clerk said Mr. Read was in a meeting and could not be disturbed. I told him it was about the earl, but he said if I didn't leave, he would have me arrested."

"Right, we need to act without delay. Is the hackney still outside?" Dominic asked.

"Yes, sir."

"Good. Come on, we are returning to Bow Street."

"I am coming too," Patricia said.

"Oh, most certainly you are," Dominic said grimly. "And on the way, you can tell me exactly what has been going on and why I have heard nothing about it."

Patricia's step faltered for the briefest of moments. "You are not going to be happy with anything but the full story, are you?" she asked, pulling on her gloves and accepting her bonnet from the stony-faced butler.

"No, I want to know it all."

"I thought so," she groaned as they left the house.

Getting access to James Read at Bow Street was not easy, even for Dominic, but Patricia took control when she saw Dominic was getting nowhere.

"If you want to be blamed for the delay in rescuing a kidnapped earl, then so be it. But if the worst happens, I doubt it will be safe for you to even walk the streets. As for finding another position, I hope you are not responsible for any family because it is hard to watch someone you love starve. So let your nonsensical actions be on your head."

The clerk had paled, and when Patricia finished, he silently stepped to one side. The fact that she had not ranted at him, just spoken clearly but gravely, made the threats seem all the more serious.

As they passed him, Patricia patted his arm. "I am sorry. If it was not the worst situation imaginable, I would have abided by the rules."

As Dominic knocked on James's door, he smiled at Patricia. "I could curse you to the devil for not telling me of Samuel's suspicions, but that was well done. I wanted to punch the man, but your way was far more efficient."

James opened the door, clearly annoyed that he had been disturbed, but he paused, the rebuke he was about to utter dying on his lips when he saw the three faces before him.

"Mr. Read, we have a problem. Lord Bentham has been attacked and taken aboard the *Fearless*," Dominic said.

"Why in all that is holy did he put himself in danger?" James demanded, stepping back and letting the three enter his office.

There was a gentleman who had been seated in the office, but at Dominic's words, he stood. "The *Fearless*, you say?"

"Yes," Dominic answered.

"Before we get ahead of ourselves, I would like to know who I am speaking to," James said dryly.

"My apologies," Dominic said. "I am Dominic Leaver and a good friend of Samuel's. This is my sister Patricia and one of Samuel's footmen who tried to raise the alarm here but was sent away."

James nodded to Terrence. "I can only say that my clerk was acting under my orders, and I am sorry he did not listen. You had better tell me exactly what happened."

Terrence did as he was bid, giving all the details in a concise way. When he had finished, James turned to the gentleman who had been listening to the footman intently.

"I think we are going to need a ship capable of catching the *Fearless*," James said. "They must have set sail by now. Mr. Leaver, Miss Leaver, this is Colonel Bannerman of the East India Company."

"And someone who is not impressed when one of his captains is not only involved with theft, but assaulting and kidnapping an earl. My carriage is outside. We will need to see which other ship is ready to sail. The faster we start the chase, the better."

"Will we catch them?" Patricia asked.

"We certainly will, Miss Leaver, and if Captain Barbosa tries anything untoward to try and avoid capture, he will find out I am not averse to using guns to drive my message home. We will return as soon as we can."

"I am coming with you," Patricia said.

"A potential gunfight and boarding of a hostile ship is not the place for a young woman."

"My betrothed is in danger and hurt. I am coming with you, Colonel, and nothing will persuade me otherwise."

"I would give in, sir," Dominic said. "We are likely to find her clinging to the side of whatever ship you decide on if you continue to refuse."

"On your head be it," the colonel said, leading the way out of the office. "But do not expect anyone to tend to you with smelling salts or the like if it gets to be too much and you faint away."

Dominic gave Patricia a stern look as they hurried after the colonel. "I would hold my tongue if I were you, or he might change his mind."

"And I might throw him overboard if he continues to be so condescending! How insulting! I will show him! I have never fainted in my life and I do not intend to start now."

"I can see why Bentham chose you." James chuckled, bringing up the rear. "I can already tell how well you are suited. He needs a woman who will not stand for his nonsense, nor pander to him."

Patricia blushed that she had been overheard, but she could not help but smile at James. "I most certainly will not. But I am not convinced he is fully aware of that quite yet."

HE JUST WANTED the movement to stop. There was nothing left in his stomach, but it continued to complain bitterly every time there was the slightest motion. As for his head, he did not think he was being too dramatic to believe that it might actually explode with the pain he was feeling.

Lying in the darkness, he tried to place the unfamiliar sounds around him while trying to ignore the smells of the place. Breathing through his mouth only helped a little, his stomach roiling as each wave of nausea hit him. In an effort to distract himself, he tried to remember how he had ended up in this hellhole.

He was to come to the conclusion that thinking was vastly over-rated as it made his head hurt even more. Knowing that something was badly amiss was not enough of a motivation for him to try to fight the darkness that threatened him. Eventually, he surrendered to the overwhelming urge to sleep. It was better that way, as then the pain and sickness eased.

He had no idea how long he had been unconscious, when he was wakened by a blinding light. Wincing and trying to shield his eyes from the piercing pain, only to find his hands were tied, he managed to croak out, "My head."

"The poor lord has a headache, does he? Perhaps that will teach you to keep your nose out of things that are none of your concern."

Samuel knew the voice. He tried to think beyond the pain in his head and frowning in concentration, he started to remember. "You are the thief. I knew something was not right about you," he said, his voice thick and gravelly and eyes still firmly closed.

"Well done. I suppose I should give you credit for that. Though what you intended to achieve by lying in wait for me, I fail to understand."

"An end to the thefts, perhaps?" Samuel could not prevent the hint of sarcasm in his tone.

"A pity your interference is causing us a problem."

"Where am I?"

"On the way to China."

"What?" Samuel exploded, trying to get up, but a searing pain in his temple caused him to fall back with a sickening groan. He was struggling with panic at the thought that Patricia would not know what had happened to him. That she would think he had deserted her made him angrier than he ever had felt before—which was a feat indeed, considering the type of mother he had.

"Yes, your darling spinster is not going to have the wedding day she longs for, after all. It was pitiful to see how besotted she was with you. I wonder if she will think you have disappeared because you could not face the prospect of life with her? I am sure society will think that, for they were surprised that the Long Meg had managed to finally capture a husband. At least, so the gossips were eager to say," Juliet taunted. She was clearly enjoying having the upper hand; there was none of the forced niceties she had spouted when in the drawing rooms of the *ton*.

"She would never think that," Samuel snapped, but there was the heavy weight of guilt in his chest that not only would she think he had left her, but he would also have caused her discomfort at the speculation society would inevitably make.

"I suppose you will find out the truth when you return—if you return—because we will certainly not be returning for years. We have yet to decide what to do with you, but I would accept you will not be seeing the shores of England anytime soon, if at all."

"Did you have any feelings for Dominic, or was that part of your masquerade?" Samuel finally managed to open his eyes, and though he did not study his surroundings in great depth, he could see that there was only one way in and out of the tiny space.

"It was nice to play the heiress for once." Juliet shrugged. "It is tedious acting the servant, being ordered around by the lazy of the world. I wanted to punish them for the things they demanded of their staff, all day, every day, but I did not wish to hang, so I took what I needed and left them to their spoiled lives."

"That is how you did it? Changing your role every time?" Samuel could not help being curious as to how she had not been recognised in society if she was constantly passing herself off as someone of wealth as Frederick had tried to do.

"Yes, a scullery maid, friend, lover, kitchen maid—whatever role would give me access to the houses without any suspicion landing on me."

"Until now," Samuel said with some satisfaction, which made Juliet laugh.

"What have you done but cause problems for yourself? I still have the necklace—and very pretty it is too—and I am in no danger of being caught. Whereas you, on the other hand..."

Samuel was tempted to tell her that the necklace was fake, just to wipe the smug expression off her face, but wisely kept his mouth shut. He was already in a precarious position, there was no point poking his captor. Not yet, anyhow.

A movement behind Juliet made her turn slightly. There was an old sailor waiting behind her. "Bates, make sure no one else sees or speaks to him," she instructed. "I don't want him to intimidate any of them into helping him."

"Aye, miss. What about food and drink?"

"Give him the bare minimum. I do not want him to be unconscious with starvation when we decide his fate. He needs to be fully aware of what is happening, or there will not be any fun in it."

Bates nodded, and she handed him the lantern before leaving without a backwards glance in Samuel's direction.

When Juliet was out of sight, Bates looked at Samuel. "I will return with food and drink. If you don't do anything foolish, we will get on just fine."

"I have no other choice but to comply," Samuel said grimly.

"That's the spirit. I will be back soon."

Samuel had no idea how long it was before the sailor returned. He was still slipping in and out of consciousness, which was a surprise as he was lying on sacks that were decidedly uncomfortable and smelled vile. In his situation, he had to be grateful that at least he was not lying on just wooden planks. The way his body was aching, that would have been torture.

When the door opened and the lantern was placed on the floor, the sailor went into the corridor and returned with a tankard and plate. "It won't be as fine as yer used to, but it will keep body and soul together."

Samuel looked askance at the plate while Bates removed the rope which tied his hands together. The lump of bread looked days old, and the cheese looked unappealing. "Are you sure about that? I think there is more chance of my dying of poisoning if I eat that."

Bates laughed. "I am glad to see you still have spirit. That is going to serve you well."

Samuel accepted the plate and tankard and took a drink. It was small beer, but it was welcome to his parched throat.

Bates nodded with approval before lowering his voice and starting to speak. "I have no gripe with you, so take heed of everything I say, and you will be the better for it."

"How do I know I can trust you?" Taking a bite of the cheese, Samuel grimaced and put the plate on the floor.

With a rueful shake of the head at Samuel's action, Bates continued. "I'm an old salt and have seen many things, but this captain and his daughter lead by fear, which isn't right. No one dares cross them, for if they do, they don't live very long afterwards."

"And no one has thought to rise against them as a group?"

"Oh, many of us have, every day, but they have their faithful ones aboard, and they are number enough to be able to fight back."

"You could swap ships."

"Some manage it, but we are watched when we're in port. They don't like losing sailors because their reputation is so bad that the word is finally out about the realities of life onboard, and so no one wants to join us."

"You sound as if you are little more than prisoners."

"Aye, we are, but that doesn't mean I have to do all that I'm bid without question."

Samuel looked at the sailor. He must be about forty years old but looked older. Brown, weather-beaten skin was criss-crossed with deep lines. He stooped as he walked, shoulders permanently hunched by life in confined ships. For some reason, whether it was because he did not have much choice or purely that he believed the man's words, Samuel was inclined to trust him. But from what he said, one aspect of his captivity became clear.

"I am not going to reach China, am I?" he asked.

"No, Miss Barbosa is desperate to get rid of you. All her talk is just to taunt you into thinking you will be her prisoner until we reach China. She has decided to end it before we reach the first port; I think she is worried you would escape somehow."

"So, I am to die here?" Samuel asked. "I must say, I had hoped my last breath would be taken in more comfortable surroundings."

Bates chuckled. "That would not cure her thirst for making people suffer," he said. "If they ask, say you can't swim."

"But I can," Samuel replied.

"Then you would likely be hanged from the yardarm. If you say you can't swim, they will send you over the side. That is the way she prefers, and it gives you a slightly better chance at surviving, though not a guarantee. I know it is a small chance. You will just have to hope there are ships close by to rescue you from the water."

"Good God, she enjoys watching people die? She is truly evil."

"Oh yes, she is. She loves finding someone's weakness and using it to her advantage. Now don't think I'm trying to bamboozle you when I say you need to give me your boots."

"What?" Samuel spluttered.

"How do you think you'll fare with those heavy boots when you need to swim for your life?"

"I am hardly likely to be able to swim long enough to reach any-where. It would be quicker to sink without trace."

"Never thought a lord would be the type to give up without a fight."

Samuel thought of Patricia, how she made him laugh, the way she had always welcomed him, made him feel part of their family, and looked at him in a way she never looked at anyone else. How she made him look forward to a happy future, something he had never thought possible. He needed to see her to explain what a fool he had been, to see her glower at him and curse him to the devil, which he knew she would, no matter how relieved she was that he was safe. The thought of never seeing her face light up when he entered a room made him ache with longing. He had to do anything he could to survive so he could get back to her. She was the best thing that had ever happened to him, and Bates was right; he was not about to give up, not when it meant he would never see her again. He would return to her, or die trying.

"No, I am not going to just accept my fate, but I will need help getting my boots off."

Though the nausea made any movement a real struggle, and the space to move was small, they eventually managed to relieve him of his highly prized top boots. Both were breathing heavily after the chore.

"I am sorry to part ways with those," he said, trying to distract himself from the nausea bubbling up inside him. He was now painfully aware that taking a bite of the cheese had been a bad idea, as his stomach heaved.

"If you get out of this fix, then I'm sure you can afford another pair," Bates said. "I had best leave you be. I have duties to attend, and these boots need hiding."

"Are you going to get into trouble? I do not wish to secure my escape at the cost of your life."

Bates shook his head while picking up the lantern. "No need to worry about me. I've had a good inning."

"You are not quite at death's door yet!" Samuel could not explain his reasoning, but he needed this man to survive whatever they were going to face.

"Don't you worry about me. It isn't going to be easy getting you off this ship alive, but they've gone too far this time. I can't just stand by and watch another innocent lose his life. There is a bond between sailors—we look out for each other—and our captain should want to protect us as much as the ship. Only this captain and his daughter have never acted with any appreciation for what we do for them. Capturing you is the last straw for me, and I don't care if I'm keelhauled for it, though I would rather not be." Bates smiled.

"Then I thank you," Samuel said as Bates nodded and left the room.

Chapter Fifteen

HOURS PASSED. ALL Samuel could do was drift in and out of sleep. It was almost pitch black in the space he was being held. A few tiny gaps in the wood gave no real light nor any suggestion as to what was happening outside the room. He had to be in the bowels of the ship by the way the outer walls curved, but beyond that, there were few clues.

When the door was unlocked, he sat up, though the light was blinding. He was relieved to see Bates entering the room.

"Glad to see you survived so far," Bates said, handing him a tankard.

"Thankfully, I had the uneaten food to help keep the rats at bay," Samuel replied. "I could have done with my boots to kill the blasted creatures."

"Ah yes, forgot about that. Oh well, they don't mind our food."

"How long have we been afloat?"

"A couple of days. You were fit for nothing when they first brought you aboard. I am impressed you survived."

"Blast it, we are further away than I hoped."

"No need to worry about that for now. I suggest you try and eat this," he said, handing Samuel a plate. "You should find it to your taste. I persuaded Cook to give you some of the captain's breakfast."

Samuel laughed. "You really are a rogue. I was considering offering you a position if we managed to get out of here alive, but I am not sure I want to now. Goodness knows what chaos and rebellion you would cause."

Bates smiled a toothless grin. "Unless you have a boat, I would be no good to yer," he said. "My life is on the sea."

They both looked up on hearing a commotion from the deck. There was shouting, then the sound of heavy boots running joined the noise.

"Do not tell me that reaction is because the captain has had a smaller breakfast?" Samuel asked, trying to lighten the mood; both of them had tensed at the activity.

"No, at least I hope not. I'd best check," Bates said. About to step out the door, he paused and came back into the room. "Take this and hide it well," he said, handing over a small blade.

Samuel accepted the weapon and, after much deliberation, put it on the inside of his stocking. It was more visible there, or at least had more chance of being seen, but he did not wish to risk putting it into his frock coat in case he was forced to take that off. There was no sign of the pistols he had had in his coat pockets or his purse. He had obviously been searched and could not risk a knife being discovered if they thought him unarmed.

The sounds of shouting and running footsteps continued for some time. He had no idea what was going on, and the lack of information had him gritting his teeth in frustration. The sea was no rougher than it had been so far, so he did not think the ship was in danger of sinking, but the commotion was going on for so long it could only be something serious.

Eventually, the door was flung open, and a furious Juliet stood in the doorway. "I knew I should have had you killed on the dockside," she spat at him.

"I am afraid you have the advantage over me. I have no idea what I could have done to have you wishing for my demise," Samuel said, giving an impression of languid indifference.

"Get him on his feet and make sure his hands are tied tightly. People like him are taught to swim," Juliet instructed.

Bates entered the room and pulled Samuel to his feet. Fiddling with the ropes around his wrists, he made it look as if he was pulling the rope tight but, in fact, he was keeping the knots as loose as possible.

"Bring him on deck." Juliet stormed away while Bates moved a lot slower. Samuel had not stood up since being on the dockside, and along with the movement of the ship, he needed the support of the other man to shuffle along the corridor.

"What has happened?" Samuel asked on a whisper.

"It seems you have friends in high places," Bates whispered back.

Curious to find out what was going on and feeling hopeful for the first time since he had been brought onboard, Samuel tried to make his legs move faster. Climbing up the steps to the deck with his hands tied was a challenge that he managed eventually, but he had to look down with closed eyes when he reached the top. The day was cloudy, but it was still brighter than anything he had seen for days, and his head started to pound once more.

"Bring him here," Juliet commanded, standing to the starboard side of the ship. "Show them he is alive."

Through watery eyes, Samuel could make out another ship bearing down on them.

"Who is that?"

"Another East India ship," Bates said.

"Shut up!" Juliet snapped at the sailor. "Or you'll be going overboard too."

Samuel and Bates exchanged a look. It seemed Juliet was determined to get rid of him, even though they were being chased.

"What do the flags mean?" he asked as the other ship raised a number of different standards.

"That they are interfering in something that has nothing to do with them," Juliet snapped.

"Prepare to be boarded," Bates said quietly.

"If they think we would give up so easily when we have come this far, they have seriously underestimated my father."

"But it is the same company as yours. It could be a mere coincidence," Samuel said conversationally.

"If you believe that, it is no wonder it took you so long to work out what I was doing," Juliet mocked. "Set the plank up."

Samuel stared at her incredulously. "Please tell me you are not going to make me walk the plank? I feel as if this is some kind of gothic pirate novel. I am surprised you could not be more original. It is very disappointing to find out that you are nothing out of the ordinary."

Juliet flushed at the words. "I would like to shoot you now, but if I throw you overboard, they will focus on saving you while we sail off into the distance. It seems you have come in useful after all."

"I am glad I could be of service," Samuel said with a slight bow.

"Enjoy your swim," Juliet mocked. She nodded to two sailors, who lifted Samuel onto the plank which was balanced through the ship's top rail.

Heart pounding, he looked down at the water, wondering if he would even survive the fall, let alone be able to free his hands and swim to safety. One thing was certain, however. He was not going to give Juliet the pleasure of seeing his fear. Turning towards her whilst being very careful to keep his movements slow, he smiled.

"I never did know what Dominic saw in you. Everyone said you were beautiful, whereas I just thought you were completely out of place in society. A harlot on a ship of men who hate you? That moniker suits you far better than that of something you could never be—a genteel lady."

Juliet spat at him. "Give me a gun!" she screamed at no one in particular. Everyone remained still, forcing her to run to where her father was at the helm. She picked up a rifle, loaded it and pointed it at

Samuel.

"Not one of your best ideas," Bates said from behind Samuel on the deck, which made him smile, despite the seriousness of the situation.

"Tell my girl that I love her, and I am sorry," he said to Bates.

"I am going to enjoy sending Miss Leaver a letter describing how you died pathetically before disappearing into the sea, lost to her forever. Do you think she will pine away, mourning you, or will she find someone like Frederick to satisfy her?"

"Oh, get on with it, woman!" Samuel shouted. "This is tedious."

There was a loud boom, and Samuel lost his footing as the whole ship shuddered. Hearing the whistle of a ball of shot passing his head, he helplessly floundered mid-air before plunging into the cold depths far below the ship.

His last thought as he disappeared beneath the waves was that he was sure he had heard Patricia scream.

Three days earlier

PROCURING A SHIP to chase after the *Fearless* was not as easy as Patricia had hoped. One ship, *Larkins*, could catch up with the *Fearless* but was not quite ready to sail and then, to add to their frustration, the tide was against them. To make matters worse, the captain was reluctant to set sail at night.

Dominic had forced Patricia to accompany him to an inn which was suitable for a lady to visit; most of the inns near the docks were places a respectable young woman should never find herself, especially at night. Hiring a private room, he had watched her with some concern as she paced back and forth.

"Why did he go to the docks? Why not wait for Mr. Read?" she asked for the twentieth time in the same number of minutes.

Her question was not necessarily aimed at Dominic, but he answered her anyway. "You will have plenty of time to find out when we reach the *Fearless*."

"Will we, though? What if they have sailed too far away?"

"The colonel seemed convinced they could be intercepted. I doubt he would embark on a fool's errand if he was uncertain of success," Dominic reasoned. "More importantly, I think you need to tell me what is really going on between Samuel and yourself."

Patricia looked at him in surprise before finally sitting down. "You might be angry when you hear the truth."

"I doubt that very much."

Sighing, she squared her shoulders. The three of them had been friends for so long, she would hate for something to spoil it, but she had to tell him everything and hope he understood why there had been some secrecy. She had already told him about Juliet. He had been quiet throughout, not revealing anything to her through words or expression. Now it was time to make her own confession about Samuel. If nothing else, it would hopefully take his mind off his own heartache.

"Though the engagement was false to start with," she said, "we both came to the conclusion that we wanted our attachment to be real. However, we have only just sorted everything out between us. My foolish words really upset him."

"I see," Dominic said, obviously amused at her discomfort.

"I would like your blessing, Dominic, but I am of age, and I love him."

"I am fully aware of how strong your feelings are for him."

"You are?" Patricia finally met his gaze and saw a mixture of amusement and smugness.

"It was obvious before the engagement was even suggested that you were perfect for each other."

"But you objected to Samuel's plan!"

"Of course I did. If I had shown anything but disgust at the scheme, you would not have been so keen to make it happen. I knew you needed something to allow you both to accept what had been under your noses for years, but the constraints of friendship always held you back."

"You are going to take credit for our making a real match of it?"

"Of course I am. Come on, you might have had to convince everyone else that your feelings were new and the attachment sudden, but I knew they had been there for goodness knows how long."

"Grandmamma never truly believed the engagement. I wonder if she suspected, the same as you?"

"Oh, damn and blast it! Grandmamma!" Dominic exclaimed.

"I never gave her a thought," Patricia said with a grimace. "We cannot leave without sending a note to her. She would be sick with worry if we just disappeared."

Dominic stood and walked to the desk, then pulled a drawer open and took out a sheet of paper. He scribbled a short, concise note, and once it had been given to the innkeeper for delivery, he sat down once more.

"I am not sure whether I wish I could see her face when she reads the letter or if I am thankful I am away," Patricia said.

Dominic grinned. "I like living. I am more than happy to be a distance away."

Patricia looked at her brother, a frown marring her features.

"What is it?" Dominic sighed in defeated resignation.

"You are more cheerful than I would expect you to be after everything I have revealed about Juliet," she answered gently.

"Would you rather I hide away, sobbing into my pillow, prostrate with grief?"

"No, but I had thought you were very attached to her. You said you thought she was the one for you."

"I thought she was, and I am probably still in love with her, though it is clear that she was just using me to gain access to the necklace," Dominic confessed. "In all honesty, at the moment, I am more angry than anything else."

"She fooled us all."

"Didn't she just? I have been a complete nodcock, I am fully aware of that. All I can concentrate on now is bringing her to justice, especially after what she has done to Samuel."

"You wish to see her hang? For that is what she faces if we do catch up to them."

Rubbing his hands over his face, he grimaced at her. "No, not when I think about it seriously, but what is the alternative? She escapes, and Samuel's dead body washes up on some distant shore?"

"Oh, do not even consider that!" Patricia choked out.

"I am sorry to upset you, but if we want Samuel back, she has to be caught and brought to justice."

"I just hate that you have been hurt as a result of all this."

"I will survive."

They were interrupted by the arrival of James Read. "The ship will sail in two hours," he said. "I have taken the liberty of ordering some food. It might be the last chance we have for a decent meal for a while, so be sure to indulge." The slight smile which accompanied his words did not soften the strain on his face.

"Good idea," Dominic said.

"Do you think we have a chance of reaching them? They have had such a good start on us," Patricia asked.

"We have the element of surprise," James said. "They have no idea that the Earl's abduction was witnessed by Terrence. If he had not accompanied Samuel, it could have been days before we knew he was missing and even longer to work out what had happened to him if we ever did find out."

"We will find him," Dominic said, touching Patricia's hand as trays of food were brought in.

"How will he be rescued from the ship?"

"As Colonel Bannerman is absolutely livid that they are misusing one of his ships for their own purposes, he is willing to fire on them to make them comply with his orders."

Patricia paled at James's words, making Dominic laugh. "If you were trying to reassure my sister, you have done a very poor job of it."

"And if you thought the inadequate note you sent was the way to inform me you were about to put yourselves in danger, then you should look at your own actions before taking someone else to task."

The formidable woman stood in the doorway, hands on hips, looking angrier than either sibling had ever seen her. This did not bode well, for in person, she was a force to be reckoned with, and they knew, without doubt, that she would not agree with their plans.

"Grandmamma," Dominic said with an audible curse.

"The only one you have, and she is absolutely furious with you both."

"Oh lord!" Dominic moaned.

"Do not think you will be able to talk me out of leaving on the ship. He is in danger, and I am going to him," Patricia said before her grandmother could start objecting.

Enid looked at her with something akin to admiration. "I see you have given up that sham of an act."

"I do not understand," Patricia responded.

"Of course you do. I knew from the start that the engagement was some sort of ruse, which was ridiculous as the pair of you have been besotted with each other for years."

Dominic burst out laughing at Enid's words. "I always thought you must be omniscient. Now I know it to be true."

Enid smiled. "I am surprised you ever doubted it."

"My mistake. I will not doubt you in the future."

"Wait a moment," Patricia said, hands on hips. "If you were of that mind, why the devil were you forcing Frederick on me at every opportunity?"

"One of you needed some sort of push to grasp that you were already in love with each other. You seemed incapable of sorting it out without some interference. And mind your language, young lady. Just because you are about to become Lady Bentham, that does not give you the right to curse."

Patricia blushed but still looked furious. "And what if I had chosen Frederick over Samuel in order to please you?"

"You would have never accepted that flash cove. I knew he was some sort of fraud from the moment he introduced himself. But I saw immediately how he could be useful, so allowed his ridiculous claims to go unchallenged," Enid explained.

"Flash cove?" Dominic spluttered. "Grandmamma, you never cease to amaze me."

"And your lack of manners never ceases to disappoint me," Enid said. "Who is this person who, from the look of him, has been laughing at our expense." She turned her attention to James, who immediately stood in order to be formally introduced.

"It is a delight to meet you, Mrs. Leaver," James said, bowing. "I take it you intend sailing with us?"

"Of course. I am glad to see you have your wits about you, unlike these two."

"Grandmamma, you cannot!" Patricia exclaimed.

"You are always quick to point out that you are of age. Well, so am I," Enid said to a further guffaw from Dominic. He was enjoying this whole situation far too much in Patricia's mind, but Enid continued without comment at Dominic's laughter. "There is nothing you can say or do that will prevent me from accompanying you. And—" she raised a hand to stop Patricia from interrupting "—if you start to spout that it will be dangerous, you, my dear, will be prevented from going, whether you are of age or not."

Patricia sat heavily on a chair while Dominic chuckled. "I think you have been bested, Patricia."

"Do not think you are in any less trouble than she is," Enid warned.

"You cannot roast me," Dominic said easily. "I am suffering from a broken heart."

Enid narrowed her eyes. "You had better explain everything. You can thank me later for bringing a portmanteau with everything we will need for a few days away."

James still looked amused but indicated the food on the table. "This diversion has lifted my spirits in a way that a whole week away from Bow Street would not have achieved. But can I suggest we concentrate on eating our fill, as we will have to leave before too long."

Enid moved over to the table. "We can talk in between eating. I can see there is still a lot I do not know."

"Dread the thought that there might actually be something you are not aware of," Patricia responded, earning herself a glare in response.

There was no other choice than to explain in more detail everything that had happened. Enid sat in silence as Dominic spoke while James watched in some amusement, tucking into the food which the others had little interest in.

At the end of his speech, Dominic shrugged. "You now know as much as we do."

Enid glanced at Patricia. "We will be having a conversation about family loyalties and extra guests in the house of which no one was aware."

Before Patricia could respond, James interjected, "I am afraid it was I who insisted on secrecy."

"Do not think I have failed to grasp that. My questions to you are about putting young women at risk when you had no idea who you were dealing with," Enid said, eyes flashing.

"I left my salad days behind me a long time ago," Patricia interrupted.

"And that is exactly the type of ninnyhammer comment that proves what a green girl you are."

"I do not think either of us is going to win this argument," James said to Patricia.

"You will quickly learn that no one ever pits themselves against Grandmamma and wins," Dominic said.

"Have you ever considered working for Bow Street?" James asked Enid, a glint in his eye.

Chapter Sixteen

S AILING FAST, EVEN through the calmest of waters, was an experience Patricia found invigorating and frightening in equal measure. She had never been aboard a ship before, having barely left the south of the country, let alone ventured abroad, so to see the land disappearing would have been something to enjoy if they had not been racing to try and save Samuel. The few days they had been sailing seemed to drag, but she knew everyone was pushing hard to make headway while they could.

The fact that the colonel was on board with the rest of the crew had an effect on the sailors. There was an unacknowledged air of tension, and the usual banter between the men working so closely together was absent. Then again, the need for speed also kept the sailors constantly busy and focusing on making the most of the wind while they had it.

Standing by the rail, Patricia let the breeze blow through her hair. Her bonnet had been discarded almost as soon as the ship had set sail, otherwise it would have been lost the moment they moved out of the estuary and they were no longer sheltered by land.

James joined her at the rail. "We will catch them, but probably not as fast as you would wish."

"They have had a good start on us."

"True, but it is not an insurmountable one. The *Larkins* was chosen for her abilities."

"I just feel so helpless," Patricia admitted. "I understand that must sound silly coming from a woman who has little control over what happens to her, but this is far worse than being reliant on family for my upkeep."

"I can understand your frustration. I very often feel as if I am in some strange world in which crime will continue even after I am old and wrinkled, more than I am already. It feels as if I work long hours, but there is no actual impact. I rarely feel in control of the domain I supposedly am in charge of."

Patricia smiled at his self-deprecating manner. "I am sure you are making a real difference."

"That is kind of you to say. Just do not let the wider populace know how I feel or I will be thrown out of my job. And I am trying to do something positive, though it is not always easy."

"It is reassuring to know that you care about those who have been forced into actions that only desperation has driven them to. Samuel was touched by your concern for the family who had been treated so ill."

James chuckled at her words. "A few months ago, he would not have done that. You are aware of the fact, aren't you?"

"Done what?"

"Gone out of his way to such an extent. You have had a good influence on him. It is nice to see he has a softer, more compassionate side."

"I know he is a good master. I am surprised you would think him otherwise," Patricia defended Samuel.

"I am sure he is good to those under his care. From what I hear, the estate is being run as well as it was when his father was alive. But I am talking about empathy for those beyond his immediate circle."

"I am not sure I can claim any credit for his change in thinking, but I am glad that he wished to help. It gave us the clue we were so desperate for."

"It certainly did. I, for one, am thankful for that alone. It will be interesting to learn what else the Barbosas have been up to."

They lapsed into a comfortable silence, Patricia wishing for the weather to remain to their advantage so they could maintain their speed. The thought of Samuel being injured or worse made her more nauseous than any motion of the ship so far.

When the "Ship Ahoy!" call was heard late the following afternoon, the activity onboard, which had been busy before, dramatically increased. As the colonel gave the order for the guns to be readied, Enid and Patricia looked at each other in consternation.

"It is just a precaution," Dominic said, approaching them. "The captain has suggested you might wish to remain below decks."

"I am staying here," Patricia said. "I need to know what is going on."

"I said that would be your response, so he asked if you would remain aft. The further away you are from any risk, the better it is for us all."

"We will not cause any problems," Enid promised. "But I agree with Patricia. It would be torture to hear what was going on without knowing if it was a good sign or not."

"Is there a telescope we could use to view the other ship?" Patricia asked.

"I will ask," Dominic answered.

The *Fearless* was not showing any sign of slowing down, even when the flags indicated the ship chasing them intended to board them.

With numerous telescopes aimed in the direction to see what was unfolding on the *Fearless*, tension increased when those watching saw Samuel appear on the deck.

"He looks ill, and his hands are tied together, but he is alive! Oh, thank God! I was afraid to hope but feared the worst," Patricia relayed to Enid, wiping her eyes before once more putting the telescope to her eye. "Oh, no! There seems to be some sort of altercation going on. What can they be intending? We cannot have come this far to not be able to reach him. I cannot bear this!"

When the plank was balanced on the railings of the *Fearless*, the captain of the *Larkins* shouted to gun number one to prepare to fire. Trying to watch what was happening to Samuel became more difficult when Patricia's hands shook on hearing the command.

"Why is he arguing?" she muttered to herself, able to interpret the expression on Samuel's face. "He always has to have the last blasted word."

"Your language leaves a lot to be desired," Enid scolded.

"Blame my betrothed," Patricia responded. "Oh! He is being helped onto the plank! His hands are still tied! Juliet is pointing a gun at him! How can she shoot him when he is so at her mercy! She is going to kill him!"

"Fire!" The captain shouted, and the ship shook slightly as the heavy cannon bounced back on its fittings, spewing the cannonball across the waves. From the moment the cannon was fired, events seemed to take place in slow motion, with everyone on the ship transfixed by the unfolding scene, helpless to do anything more than watch and hope.

The cannonball hit its target, sending wood flying in all directions as it made a hole in the side of the *Fearless*. The impact caused the loosely secured plank to lurch dangerously, with Samuel struggling to stay on it. It was clear he was losing the battle. And when the crack of a gunshot rang out, Samuel fell into the sea.

THE SEAWATER ENGULFED him as the shock of the cold took his breath away. Fighting to stem the panic overwhelming him, he struggled to kick his feet to try to stop his downward motion.

The fine wool of his frock coat, admired by many, now worked against him, becoming a dead weight as the water soaked into the material.

Samuel knew he had little time to reach the surface before his lungs emptied of air. Wriggling to grab the knife which had thankfully not been discovered, he worked in the eerie silence of the water, with only a little light filtering down.

Desperately trying not to drop the knife, he cut at the ropes. Bates had most certainly saved his life by loosening the knots, but even so, blood floated around him as he hacked at his hands.

He had no choice but to hold onto the blade while trying to slice the ropes. When his hands were freed, he let the knife fall into the watery depths, and kicking his legs to try and force his body towards the surface, he clawed at his frock coat, trying to get out of it.

Feeling his energy fading as the burning in his chest increased due to lack of air, he finally released himself from the dead weight and, with one last push, looked towards the light streaming above him.

He burst through the water, spluttering and coughing; his lungs felt on fire. If he thought his troubles were over, his precarious situation was brought home once more as he floundered, choking on the salt water he inhaled when trying to catch his breath.

The ships had not sailed far away from him, and when he managed to stop choking, he looked towards the *Fearless*, unsure of what he would face next.

Juliet was leaning over the rail watching him, anger clear on her expression; she seemed older and harsher somehow. She was an excellent actress to have fooled them all, he mused as he tried to guess what she was thinking. He could see Bates was near her. Samuel did not take his eyes off Juliet but tried to move backwards to put more distance between himself and the ship. This close, he was still vulnerable.

His fear was proved well-founded when Juliet raised her gun and pointed it at him. Expecting to hear a crack as she fired, he was startled instead by another boom of cannon fire from behind him.

This ball hit the *Fearless* directly in the midship, sending wood flying in all directions. Samuel had kept his eyes on Juliet, and at the same time as the cannon had been fired, Bates had lunged for the gun Juliet was holding. With the cannonball's impact, Bates lost his footing and fell overboard, still clutching the gun.

"Blast it. Why sailors do not learn how to swim is beyond me," Samuel muttered to himself, striking out to swim to Bates. "That man has got a damned death wish."

Bates was hanging onto a splintered piece of wood by the time Samuel reached him. He was also doggedly clinging to the rifle.

"I do not think that will offer much protection," Samuel said through chattering teeth.

"I suppose not," Bates said with a slight smile before letting the gun sink into the water.

"It seems I have you to thank for saving my life for the second time."

"I refuse to be sent to the gallows because of them," Bates said, gesturing toward the *Fearless*. "Although I don't fancy drowning either."

"No, me either. Why are they not firing back?" Samuel asked. His arms felt like dead weights, and he was feeling even more exhausted than before he had surfaced. He really should be concentrating on swimming to the other ship.

"Are you feeling well?" Bates suddenly asked. "Your lips are blue."

Samuel grabbed another piece of wood from the *Fearless* as it bobbed by. "I am so cold." His teeth continued to chatter.

"Do not let go of that wood," Bates said as cannon fire sounded behind them. "Looks as though the *Fearless* is fighting back after all." They both ducked instinctively, though they were in no danger from the cannon.

The volley from the *Fearless* caused the rescue ship to release a full-scale attack. This had the effect of showering Samuel and Bates with debris.

Bates cried out in pain. "My blasted arm! Are your rescuers trying to kill us?" he demanded, wincing when he saw the large splinter of wood protruding from his shoulder.

"That needs to come out," Samuel said, moving as if to pull it.

"Oh no ye don't! Leave it be," Bates snapped at him. "I refuse to bleed to death. And I sure don't want to announce our presence to any sharks."

"It is not that big," Samuel said, but moved away from Bates. Just then, he heard a shout, and he sagged with relief when he saw a rowing boat approaching. "Oh, thank God," he said. Then he slipped beneath the water.

Chapter Seventeen

A few moments before…

W HEN PATRICIA SAW Samuel fall from the *Fearless*, she ran towards the front of the ship, screaming Samuel's name, only to be grabbed by Dominic before she reached the bow.

"You are not throwing yourself in!" Dominic shouted at her.

"His hands were tied!" Patricia retorted, struggling against her brother's hold.

"Look! They are lowering a boat already." Dominic said, trying to calm her. One of the boats, normally strapped to the hull, was being dropped over the side with four sailors in it.

"They will be too late!" Patricia cried, tears pouring down her face.

"They will be able to reach him before any attempt you make," Dominic said, his tone more soothing than it had been.

"He is still under the water," Patricia moaned, watching the spot where Samuel had disappeared, willing him to surface with every second that passed.

"I know." Dominic was torn between caring for Patricia and wanting to throw himself overboard to try and save his friend.

Minutes seemed to pass as they clung to each other, waiting for a miracle. When Samuel finally reappeared, coughing and choking, Patricia let out a cry of relief.

"The boat is nearly in the water," Dominic said.

"Why are they not moving quicker?" Patricia demanded, sparing only a cursory glance at the sailors working to lower the rowing boat before her eyes turned back to Samuel.

"And tip even more people into the water?" Dominic said dryly. "They know what they are doing and have probably done it countless times before. Trust them to bring him to us."

"You are no good to him being a wet goose," Enid said from behind them. "We will have no more hysterics, thank you very much. I brought you up better than that."

"Sorry," Patricia said, a half-smile peeking out despite her feelings of utter panic and complete loss of control. "I just hate feeling so helpless."

"As do we all," Enid responded.

They watched as the events unfolded. Patricia almost stuffed her fist into her mouth to prevent her from screaming when she saw Juliet pointing the gun at Samuel over the edge of the ship.

When the cannon exploded from beneath their feet, they all jumped and held their breath until they saw that it being fired had no impact on Samuel. It flew high above his head, but the impact had the desired effect when the sailor who had been standing next to Julia fell into the water, the gun she had been brandishing in his hands.

James approached the huddle. "The captain is preparing for a skirmish," he started. "The *Fearless* is not running away as they expected it to, and the captain is not about to lose Samuel or the crew he has sent after him. It is far from ideal, but Captain Barbosa cannot be allowed to successfully attack a ship. It will be dangerous and unpleasant, and the colonel and I ask you to retire to the captain's cabin to remain safe."

"But—"

"No, Patricia," Dominic said firmly. "We will be a liability if we remain on deck. You can help Samuel by removing yourself from danger and waiting until he is brought on board. Then you will be able to help him."

"After seeing how poor your taste in women is, I am impressed that you could be so sensible. Well done," Enid approved.

"Grandmamma!" Patricia exclaimed in horror at the callous words.

"I suppose she has a point," Dominic said, leading both women away with a nod to James. "I just wish she could be a little subtler about it."

"It was a compliment," Enid said.

"Barely," Dominic responded. "And it definitely held a sting within it."

"Is now not the time to offer to find you a suitable wife?" Enid asked. "I could do a far better job of it."

"There will never be a right time to suggest that," Dominic ground out. "I am completely against marriage from now on."

"Now that Patricia is to be settled, I will have to find something to fill my time. The least you could do is to let me consider who might be suitable for you at some point."

"Do not worry. Patricia will soon have a brood of children to keep you busy."

Patricia did not respond as they all stumbled when the ship shuddered with what felt like a hundred cannons firing together.

"How will the *Fearless* survive this kind of attack?" Patricia asked, surprised that she was relieved to be entering the captain's large cabin. It might be safer if they were going to suffer from a similar retaliation to what the captain was letting loose, and it certainly felt further away from the trouble, being at the back of the ship.

"That is not our concern." Dominic shrugged, but he moved away from them and sat down heavily, a troubled expression on his face.

Patricia looked as if to follow him, but Enid shook her head. "Leave him be," she said gently. "Let him have time to accept that he has had a lucky escape. It will not feel like that for a while, but eventually he will come about."

Time seemed to slow down as the three waited for news, but then Patricia stopped pacing and listened to the commotion going on outside.

"Something is different," she said, moving to the door. "The volley of fire is only one way."

"Do not think you are going anywhere to find out," Enid warned, but the cabin door opened and James entered.

"We have him," he said.

"What is wrong with him?" Patricia asked, immediately picking up on the worry in his eyes.

"It happens often," James started. "Or so the captain tells me. If someone is in the sea and they think rescue is close, it is almost as if they relax too much and sink under the water."

"He's gone?" The world seemed to tilt. After everything, had they not been able to save him? She had never felt the darkness which threatened to overwhelm her at his words.

"No! Luckily one of the sailors could swim and jumped in after him. But he is unconscious and very cold."

"I need to see him," Patricia said.

As if summoned by her words, three sailors carrying Samuel entered the room and placed him on the captain's bunk.

"He needs to get out of his clothes and be wrapped in blankets," a sailor said to James. "We have to return to help the others."

"We will attend him," James said, and the sailors left the room. "Mr. Leaver, if I could ask for your help? Ladies, if you would care to turn away for a moment whilst we get these wet clothes off him."

Enid rolled her eyes at Patricia, but they both faced away from the bunk. While James and Dominic were undressing Samuel, Patricia answered a knock on the door and accepted a bundle of blankets with shaking hands, though she was calmer now that Samuel was in relative safety.

"The captain has said to light his stove; it will help," the sailor said.

There was a small iron stove to one side of the room. It was fixed to an iron plate on the floor with a basket of wood to the side. It was the first sign of heat that Patricia had noticed on the ship, except for the cooking stove.

"Please thank the captain on his lordship's behalf," she said before closing the door.

Dominic took the blankets from her and nodded towards the stove. "Will you be able to light it?"

"I will give it a try, though I have never lit a fire before."

Enid tutted. "It is a basic skill that everyone should know."

"You should not have surrounded us with such highly efficient maids then," Patricia responded, knowing her grandmother was aiming to lighten the mood and trying to join into the spirit of it. Though the weight of terror had lifted, any levity from her was forced. Until she knew Samuel was well, she could not relax.

Within minutes Enid got the stove working. James and Dominic used all the blankets they had been given, and both had added their own thick frock coats to the pile.

"I had better go and find out what has been going on," James said when there was nothing else he could do. "The *Fearless* looked to be in bad shape when I came down here. And to make matters worse for them, the crew seemed to be fighting amongst themselves."

"I will come with you. There might be something I can help with," Dominic said.

Patricia rushed to Samuel's side, laying a hand against his cold cheek, horribly aware of how still he was. When Dominic had left the room, she distracted herself by saying, "Dominic is hurting more than he is admitting to."

"He will come about soon enough. Juliet merely bruised his heart; he is not broken-hearted no matter how much he thinks he is."

"He thought that she was the one for him. That is what he told me when he brought her to meet us. He has never introduced us to anyone else," Patricia said.

"It was an infatuation. It will do him good in the long term. He will be more circumspect in future when considering a wife. She was pretty and exotic. I think you will find he recovers sooner than you expect him to."

"I hope so." Patricia looked at Samuel's ashen face with dread. "I wish I could do something that would help him to recover. I am sick of feeling so helpless."

"Keep him warm. I doubt there is little else we can do for now," Enid said, stoking the fire.

Dominic returned to the cabin sooner than they expected. "Grandmamma, they need help. They are bringing injured sailors onboard who need attention—the ones who managed to get off the *Fearless*. Some have not been so lucky."

"Has the ship sunk?" Enid asked.

"No, it will probably limp back to port. But the ones who are loyal to the Barbosas did not make it easy for those who wanted to escape."

"Patricia, will you be able to manage alone?"

"Of course. I would help myself…"

"There is no need to feel guilty," Dominic said quickly. "If there was anything I thought I could do for Samuel, I would stay here myself. Everyone knows he needs attending to, and only because there are two of you is the captain asking for help."

Patricia nodded in thanks and was soon left alone with Samuel. Pulling a chair up to the bunk, she rested her hand on top of his pile of blankets. "Samuel, come back to me."

Chapter Eighteen

DOMINIC AND ENID re-entered the cabin a lot later. Afternoon had turned into evening, and now darkness surrounded the ship. Patricia had been supplied with extra wood for the fire and food and drink, but the sailor who brought the items was eager to leave to return to his other duties. Dominic flopped on the nearest chair, rubbing his hands over his face and groaned.

"That was grim," he said quietly. "Cannonball injuries are brutal."

"So were the wounds inflicted by the other sailors," Enid said. She was pale, and her clothing was dirty and stained.

"Grandmamma, you should have changed places with me when you saw how bad it was."

"No, child, it was best I was there. I have done more nursing than you, and it is not an insult, but you would have been distracted. How is he?"

"The same," Patricia replied despondently.

"He will rally," Dominic said.

"Would you mind if I took a walk on deck? Just for a few moments. I need to feel the fresh air," Patricia asked.

"I will accompany you," Dominic answered.

Stepping onto the deck, Patricia took a moment to take in the scene. It almost felt as if she had left one ship and boarded another. The deck was swarming with people, many of whom were injured and sitting in small groups. Some of the crew were carrying out repairs to the hull. It had not received any catastrophic hits, but there was damage. The whole scene was lit by lanterns, but the black of the night sky seemed to be pressing against the side of the ship. The only thing visible out to sea was a few lights, which she presumed belonged to the *Fearless*.

"What happened to Juliet? Is she here?" she asked Dominic.

"I am presuming she is still on the *Fearless*," Dominic answered. "She has not been brought onboard, and as far as we know, she has not tried to leave her ship."

"I am sorry it has turned out this way for you."

"I should hate her—and I think part of me does—but I am stupidly hoping she was not hurt. Ridiculous when she will be hung for what she has done."

"It would be a surprise if you were not conflicted," Patricia said. "I would hate to be in your situation; it would break my heart."

"Luckily, you chose wisely. Come, stretch your legs before we return to Samuel."

Walking around the main deck, they were approached by James, who nodded at them both. "Any news?" he asked.

"Not yet," Patricia replied.

"This situation did not turn out as expected. We thought that once they saw they were being pursued, they would surrender. It appears, however, that they thought they could get away."

"Foolish when the ship belongs to the East India Company. I cannot see Colonel Bannerman allowing anyone to secure and make off with one of his ships," Dominic agreed.

"What will happen to the *Fearless* and those still left onboard?" Patricia asked.

"They have little choice but to go to the nearest port. The damage is such that if they faced any adverse weather conditions, it would most certainly be the end of the vessel and most of those onboard. Luckily for us, the nearest port is Dover. Once we dock, Colonel

Bannerman will arrange a welcoming party for those who have been loyal to the captain by the time they eventually reach shore. We are still able to travel at speed, but he wants to keep the *Fearless* in his sights in case they try something even more foolish."

"What about those who wanted to leave and were being stopped?"

"They will be given the option of transferring to another East India ship. Bannerman said that the company has to take some responsibility for one of their captains being able to use a ship to their own ends and treating the sailors so ill. Some of these men are genuinely terrified of the repercussions they will face if the ship is returned to Captain Barbosa. He has commanded with extreme cruelty and fear."

"The poor men," Patricia said. Dominic looked pensive, and Patricia decided he had heard enough. "I would like to return to check on Samuel if that is acceptable."

"Of course." Dominic led her to the cabin without speaking further.

Enid had settled near Samuel but stood as they entered. "I think there are signs he is improving."

"Oh, thank goodness!" Patricia was immediately at Samuel's side, touching his face. "He feels warmer! At last," she sighed.

It was another hour before Samuel's eyes fluttered open. "Patricia?" he croaked.

"Yes, I am here," she answered, kissing his forehead, unable to stop touching his face, her hands gently roaming over him as if she hardly believed he was there.

"I was so cold…" Samuel shivered at the words. "But I heard you scream, and I knew I had to live."

Patricia smiled at him. "I am so glad you thought that, for I would have been very lonely without you."

"Bates?"

"Who?"

"Bates, he saved me."

"He is well and glad to be on board, though he has been worried about you," Enid said.

"I am going to force him to learn how to swim," Samuel said, drifting back to sleep.

It was not long before he awoke again. This time, Dominic helped him to sit, and Patricia poured him a cup of warming green tea. Dominic informed him of everything that had gone on, from their perspective, and then it was Samuel's turn to tell his tale.

"It seems that between them, Bates and Terrence saved your life," Dominic said.

"I am very lucky that they both thought to risk their own safety to help me."

"Bates would like to see you, if you feel up to it," Enid said.

"Of course," Samuel said.

When Enid left the room, he asked Dominic, "What time is it?"

"Very late or very early, depending on your viewpoint," his friend said. "Everyone is reluctant to go to bed, as there is so much to do. But it should not be too many hours before we reach Dover."

"Dominic, could you give me a moment with your sister, please?"

"Yes, but Grandmamma will not take long to find Bates, so do not dally."

When the door closed, Samuel held out his hands to Patricia, which she took immediately. "I truly believed that I would never see you again," he said, pulling her to him.

"I have never been more afraid," Patricia said.

"Nor I. I want to tell you something that I do not wish to remain unsaid. If anything should happen to me now or in the future, I need you to know."

"Do not speak like that. You are safe now."

"Am I? Juliet has not yet been caught, and she hated the fact that she did not kill me."

"But she will be imprisoned the moment her ship docks."

"I still wish you to know that I have never loved anyone before you. I was fond of my father, but our relationship was strained because of my mother's behaviour. And, of course, the less said about her, the better."

Patricia smiled at him. "Anyone else would scold you for having no filial affection for your parents, but having seen how they were, I completely understand. I have always been saddened that you did not have the type of relationship Dominic and I shared with our parents."

"You were very lucky to have them in your life, even for such a short time."

"I know."

"But there is no need to feel sorry for me. I have always felt that I belonged with you. Only I did not understand quite how attached I was until recently. I love you, Patricia. More than you could ever imagine. I am going to spend the rest of my days making sure you are happy."

"That sounds appealing," Patricia said with a grin.

Samuel smiled in return. "I can see that I am to have my hands full."

"Do it with the knowledge that I love and adore you too."

Samuel kissed her but was interrupted by a cough.

"Closed-door kisses," Enid said with a raised eyebrow. "We will be seeking out a clergyman the moment we dock."

"That sounds like the best plan I have heard in a long time," Samuel said. "Come in, Bates."

The sailor walked into the cabin, a toothless grin lighting up his face. "'Tis good to see yer, my lord."

"We were never so formal," Samuel said.

"'That was because yer had to be good to your gaoler."

"I hope that I am a better person than that. I need to demand something of you."

"And here's me believing ye when yer said yer weren't a lofty toff."

"Rogue," Samuel responded to Bates's laugh. "Anyway, the first is non-negotiable. You are learning to swim. If that cannonball had not struck and thrown wood into the water, you would have drowned before I could have reached you."

"I am too old to learn."

"Nonsense. If you refuse, you had better decide on what position would suit you other than being a sailor because you are staying on land."

"Is he always this way?" Bates asked Dominic.

"He certainly is. I would give in gracefully if I were you; it is often easier."

Bates turned to Samuel once more. "I know why ye are offering, and there's no need to feel obliged to me. I just did what was right."

"You risked your life more than once. I take that level of loyalty seriously."

"In that case, send me to the seaside until this arm is healed, and we will be even."

"Where do you wish to go?"

"Somewhere warm. These old bones don't like the damp."

"Come back with us, and my man of business will sort out some-where for you. Until then, you can speak to my other staff and see if they can tempt you away from the sea."

"That will never happen, but I thank yer for your hospitality. I will take yer up on that because I'm no use to anyone like this," he said, wincing as he moved his injured shoulder.

"Good, I'm glad that's settled. Thank you, Bates, for everything."

"Yer welcome," Bates responded. He turned to Patricia as he was leaving the cabin. "You've got yourself a good 'un."

"I know," Patricia said with a smile at Samuel's blush.

The four left in the room once Bates had departed were too tired to do anything other than snooze. Samuel had offered his bunk to Enid and Patricia, but they had both declined, insisting that the chairs were good enough.

Dawn had long since broken by the time they docked. There was a huge amount of activity, and although they did not see the colonel again, the party said their goodbyes to James and the captain, who recommended an inn for them to stay in, one that was suitable for the gentry.

When they arrived at the White Hart, they were led into a private room while their chambers were being prepared. Enid stood in front of the fireplace until the other three sat down.

"I have a proposition," she started.

"I am now more worried than when there were cannonballs flying over my head." Samuel grimaced, at which Dominic laughed.

"I would expect you two to be ridiculous," Enid grumbled. "I think we should send a message out to the nearest clergyman and get you two married. There is going to be enough speculation when we return home as to where we have all been. This would provide a perfect diversion."

"We have not got the documentation," Samuel said, watching Patricia for her reaction.

"That is where you are wrong. Almost the moment after you announced your supposed engagement, I sourced everything out and have carried it around with me ever since. Just in case."

"I cannot believe that you would do something so outrageous!" Patricia gasped.

"Why not? You were besotted with each other, and it was inevitable that when you spent more time together as a couple, you would finally acknowledge your feelings. I did not think it would take you quite as long as it did, though, even with my pushing Frederick forward."

Samuel shook his head at Dominic. "I now understand completely why she terrifies you."

Dominic grinned and folded his arms. "Let us see if you are brave enough to take her on."

"I am not sure I would be. But in this instance, why would I? She is offering the perfect solution as far as I can see. Unless you would rather wait?" he asked Patricia.

"But your mother?" Patricia asked.

"I am perfectly content that it would be us four. In fact, after our conversation about the type of wedding we would like, this is exactly what I want."

Patricia smiled. "In that case, we need to find a clergyman. And soon."

Chapter Nineteen

S TANDING IN THE private room in the inn, with only Enid, Dominic, Samuel, and as a last addition, James, Patricia had never felt so happy. Yes, her dress was of a practical cotton, and Samuel had only his stockinged feet, shirt and breeches, but each thought the other looked perfect.

With Patricia smiling shyly at Samuel as they exchanged their vows, the clergyman was almost an irrelevance as they committed to each other. When the short service was finished, Patricia looked at her hand, now sporting Enid's wedding ring.

"This is very kind of you," she said to Enid, who had insisted she should wear the ring.

"I cannot think of a better way of passing it on to you," Enid said sincerely. "I hope it will bring you the happiness that I shared with your grandfather."

"It is my job to make sure she is happy," Samuel said.

"You had better not fail her, she is precious to me," Enid said. "But if you have even a little of your father in you, I know she will be fine."

Samuel looked surprised. "Thank you. But I thought you had taken me in dislike when we first announced our engagement."

"That was because I knew there was something amiss, though I did not know about the thefts. I was furious with you both, but you especially."

"I am sorry for the deceit. It will not happen again."

"Good. Now, gentlemen, it is time we left these two alone. You can escort me around town for the day, and we can see how Colonel Bannerman is faring," Enid said.

Patricia flushed beet red. "Grandmamma, there is no need to go out."

"There is every need. That boy still looks fit to drop. Now be a good wife and spend a quiet day together," Enid said.

Samuel smiled as the others left. Once they were alone, he took Patricia into his arms. "She is not very subtle, but I am happy for it."

"It is so embarrassing."

"I am a little weary."

Immediately, Patricia was all concern. "Why did you not say something sooner? We could have had the marriage another day."

"And spend more time away from you? I wanted to be your husband today even more than I did before I left for the docks."

"We will be having a conversation about that at some point, but I refuse to spoil our wedding day."

"In that case, I had best keep you occupied." Holding out his hand, he took her palm and kissed it. "I want to be close to you, to make you mine, to give myself, body and soul to you, Patricia."

"I-I want that too."

"Good." Without another word, he led her from the private room and hand in hand, they entered his chamber. Closing and locking the door, he smiled at her. "Do not look so nervous."

"I cannot help it. This is completely different to tormenting you in a ballroom or even in a carriage."

"We have been in the same chamber before, and I have the memory of you standing in your nightgown imprinted on my mind. I have thought about it every night before I sleep."

"I felt foolish then, but I am afraid now. I know I should not, but that woman's words keep repeating through my head." Patricia took in a breath as he gently turned her and started to unfasten the buttons of her dress. She was afraid of spoiling the moment, but nerves were making her doubt everything that was about to happen.

"Which woman? I do not care about any other woman but you," he said, kissing along her shoulder as the dress fell from it.

"She said you needed someone experienced."

Samuel paused and pulled her back to face him. "I need you. I have only ever needed you. My affairs in the past were simply a means to seek relief, nothing more. Today, if you will allow me, I am going to make love for the first time with the only person I have ever loved."

"You have been taking lessons from Frederick on flowery speeches, have you not? You can admit it to me," Patricia teased, trying to lighten the mood. She was deeply affected by his words, but their friendship had been based on their ability to tease each other, and instinctively, she knew that it was still important.

"Minx!" he laughed, picking her up and carrying her to the bed. "I am far better than he is, for my words are heartfelt and true."

"You do have a habit of saying the right things at the right time," she whispered as he bent to kiss her.

"Let me show you the rest," Samuel whispered back, taking her mouth and pushing her gently onto the mattress. "I want you so much," he groaned.

Patricia relaxed at his words and the intense expression in his eyes. She had never seen this version of him, vulnerable yet powerful, and his look of longing as he lifted her dress above her head, almost with reverence, had her breath catching in her throat. She loved him; she truly loved him.

Once Samuel had undressed her and released her hair, she wrapped her arms around his neck and buried her face into his shoulder. His hands explored her body, gently stroking her, sending tingles through her and making her breath hitch as his fingers delicately teased her sensitive skin.

Pulling away from her, he smiled. "Please, do not hide your face. I want to see what you enjoy, to learn what you want me to do."

Patricia lay on the bed, her skin almost on fire with what he had already done, but there was a little mischief still lurking within her. "I would like to see my husband as undressed as I am." That her cheeks heated at the request, she ignored, especially at the wicked grin her words caused.

"Oh, my lady, whatever you wish for, I promise to give." Standing and stripping the few clothes he wore, he soon returned to the bed, pressing his body against hers.

Patricia swallowed at the sight of him, all muscular deliciousness and then met his eyes. "I want you. I do not know what I am asking for, but I know that I have a need that I have never felt before."

"Let me show you just how to satisfy that need," Samuel said, once more kissing her deeply and showing her that what she had felt so far was only the start of breathless ecstasy.

AS THE SUN disappeared beyond the horizon, Patricia snuggled into Samuel's side. His arm wrapped around her, holding her close. They were both still undressed, neither wishing to move.

"I suppose Dominic and Grandmamma will be returned by now," Patricia said sleepily. "Should we get up?"

"No."

"You could have at least thought about it for a moment before answering," she choked on a laugh.

"The choice was easy. Be here with you, your body pressed against mine, or make polite conversation. I do not believe for one moment that you want to seek them out."

"I don't," Patricia said, hiding her face again.

"Never be ashamed of wanting to spend time with me, especially in bed," Samuel said, lifting her chin and dropping a quick kiss on her lips.

"You have turned me into a doxy," she huffed. "Because I do want to stay here."

"That, my love, is music to my ears," Samuel said, pushing her back against the pillows.

"Again? I thought you said I had worn you out?"

Samuel chuckled. "When my wife says she wants to stay in bed with me, I am suddenly filled with energy."

"They will think we are shameful."

"I do not give a fig what anyone else thinks. I just want to enjoy you and give you as much pleasure as I am capable of."

Patricia thought it best to indulge her new husband, especially when his hands started to wander and her body prickled once more in anticipation. "I cannot believe I have turned into a meek wife," she moaned.

"Do not worry. I do not think it will be long before you turn into a demanding one."

"I will not!" she laughed.

"I hope you will," Samuel said, nibbling her neck. "I can see me liking that side of you a great deal." He prevented any more conversation with a deep kiss.

On waking hours later, Samuel was surprised and a little disappointed to see Patricia standing, dressed in her chemise, looking out of the window. "Come back to bed," he said, his voice hoarse with sleep.

Turning to him, she smiled sadly. "No, I do not think it would be a good idea."

Immediately on the alert, he sat up. "What is it? What's wrong."

"I cannot do this," she said, her voice cracking.

"Do what? Patricia, you are scaring me. What has changed? I do not understand." Samuel was in a panic—he had no idea what had altered since they had fallen into a deep, exhausted, but contented, sleep.

"Amelia said that I would not be able to stand seeing you with anyone else, and that was brought home with some force when I thought you were going to make a match of it with Miss Bertram. But then we got carried away."

"What has this got to do with any of that? We are married. I was never interested in Miss Bertram, you know that."

"But you said that you would likely be a poor husband, because of the example set by your parents, and I cannot bear the thought of you doing—what we have just shared—with another."

"What are you talking about? I am going to try my damndest to be a good husband!" Samuel exclaimed, running his hand through his hair.

"What has changed? You were convinced that you would be unable to be one only a few weeks ago."

"Everything has changed! How can you think that, after all we have shared? Patricia, this is not like you. Why are you so insecure? You know me. Surely you believe that I could not hurt you in such a way."

A banging on the door made Samuel curse loudly. "What is it?" he shouted when the banging continued.

"We need to speak," Dominic shouted through the door. "Urgently."

"Damn and blast it. Fine! Give us a few minutes," Samuel said, throwing the covers back. Glancing at Patricia, he nodded towards her dress which had been abandoned yesterday afternoon. "I will help you dress, but at the earliest opportunity, we are continuing this discussion."

"You will say one thing. I will believe another. Is there any point?"

"Good God! Where is my Patricia, and what have you done with her? She would not be so defeatist," Samuel muttered as he fastened buttons.

Chapter Twenty

DOMINIC WAS PACING in the private room when Patricia and Samuel joined him. Enid was already there. "We need to leave," Dominic said without preamble.

"Why?" Samuel asked.

"I have had a visit from Read. It seems Juliet and her father decided that they did not wish to hang after all. At some point in the journey back, they abandoned the *Fearless* and took one of the rowing boats."

"Good God! Can nothing be straightforward with this case?" Samuel cursed. "Are there efforts to track them down?"

"Read says that Bannerman is furious, but he has his hands full with the sailors who were loyal to the Barbosas. And with the damage to the ships, he is making arrangements to have repairs done quickly, so this episode will have no lasting impact on upcoming journeys. He has sent out word that the Barbosas are wanted, which will be passed from port to port. They never made themselves popular, so it should only be a matter of time before they turn up."

"And you think we are a target?" Patricia asked.

"When they find out the necklace is fake…" Samuel said.

"Yes, I would imagine they will hate you even more than they do now," Dominic agreed. "That is why we need to leave. I would suggest we return to your estate."

"Of course." Samuel nodded. "I will send an express, and then we can set off. I need to find footwear of some sort." He looked down at his still stockinged feet.

"I will sort that if you send the express," Dominic said.

Samuel sat and scribbled a note before leaving the room to get it sent immediately. Enid looked at Patricia with interest.

"What is going on in that head of yours?"

"Nothing. Just thinking about the Barbosas."

"You had no idea about them when you entered this room. I expected you to be unable to wipe the smile from your face, but instead, you looked troubled and distinctly unhappy."

Patricia had flushed at Enid's insinuation, but as Samuel returned to the room, she did not offer any explanation. Her grandmother was right. She should be the happiest person, but the doubts about her being a good enough wife for him had started in the early hours and had niggled their way under her skin until she had blown them out of proportion. She had managed to convince herself that he was the person who would tire of her and hurt her the most in the long run.

Years of being told she was too tall, not handsome enough and had nothing to offer a husband had been easier to ignore before, but now she had met the man she loved more than anyone and the thought of their differences tearing them apart was too much for her fragile self-esteem. Lack of sleep and the worry over Samuel had caused those thoughts to take hold and now she was unable to rein them in.

A hackney was soon obtained, and they set off from the inn, all eager to get away from the coast as soon as possible.

"We will need to stop in London, inform Mother of what we intend and encourage her to remain in town."

"Surely you would want her to accompany us?" Patricia asked.

"I need to make arrangements for the dower house to be prepared for her. When she hears that, she will definitely want to remain in London," Samuel said with a small smile.

"Is the dower house in a bad state?" Patricia asked.

"No, but it will make her feel old," Samuel said. "She is clinging to youth like I clung to that piece of wood in the water."

"I seem to recall you let go of it," Dominic pointed out.

"Exactly. Old age comes to us all."

"Speak for yourself," Enid cursed him, making them laugh for the first time since they had left.

It was a long day, even though at one of the first inns they came to, Samuel had hired the best carriage available and the fastest horses. Only stopping when necessary, it was late into the night when they arrived at the Leaver household in London.

"Will you be ready by noon to set off?" Samuel asked Dominic.

"Of course."

Patricia went to move out of the carriage, but Samuel put his hand out. "Lady Bentham, your home is with me now."

Patricia blushed but laughed. "I forgot! How stupid of me."

"It has been a long day," Samuel acknowledged, but her action had hurt him.

They continued in silence until reaching the Bentham house, and Samuel helped her out of the carriage. Putting his arm through hers, they walked to the door, opened with some surprise by the butler.

"Welcome home, m'lud. Her ladyship has been worried about you."

"Hello, Bryant. I am surprised she has even noticed."

Samuel's words received a nod. "She has been out and about as always."

"Is she out now?"

"Yes, m'lud."

"Good. Bryant, please let me introduce the new Lady Bentham to you. This is not an ideal situation, but we need to leave for Bentham House by noon tomorrow. I have sent an express, so they will be expecting us."

"My lady." The butler bowed. "Welcome."

"Thank you," Patricia responded.

"I am sorry I did not know earlier, or the household staff would have been here to welcome you."

"There is no need to distress yourself. We have been on somewhat of an adventure. Your staff would never have expected that they would have to remain up for our late arrival," Patricia said. She had known Bryant for years but was aware that their relationship would change, now that she was lady of the house.

"We can do the formal stuff when Lady Bentham is safe," Samuel said.

"Is there anything I need to be aware of?" Bryant immediately became more focused on his master.

"I need guns, and so does Lady Bentham. The small decorative pistols will be perfect for her." Noticing Patricia's surprised look, he smiled. "I am taking no risks and know you are as likely to protect me as I am you."

Patricia nodded with approval. "Of course."

"If there is anything to eat in the kitchen, I would appreciate it but do not go to any trouble. Just bread and cheese would be fine." Samuel's stomach roiled at the memory of the bread and cheese he had been served on the *Fearless*. Thankfully, his kitchen was far better supplied.

"Of course, m'lud. Her ladyship's chamber…" The poor butler was embarrassed that Samuel's mother still resided in the chamber she had occupied since her marriage, though it was rightfully Patricia's now.

"Do not worry about that. We shall sleep in my room tonight. We have the sitting room too. I will lock the door to Mother's room."

"Should I raise some of the footmen to keep guard overnight, m'lud?"

"Yes, please. Tell them they will be rewarded for their extra work."

"That is very generous of you," the butler said. "I shall bring everything you need to your room, m'lud."

"Thank you, Bryant." Samuel led the way up the marble stairs.

Patricia had visited many times but had never ventured into one of the chambers. "I am sorry that I cannot perform a tour for you. I think it is best that we remain above stairs and just in my suite."

"You are really worried about this, aren't you? Do you think she will try to reach us?"

"I saw a woman half-mad with hatred," Samuel said. "I can only imagine what she will do once she finds out the necklace is nothing but paste."

"In that case, I am glad you asked for the pistols."

Samuel opened the door to his chamber and ushered Patricia in before him. "As I promised Dominic right at the start of all this, I will do everything in my power to protect you."

"I know," Patricia said quietly. The room was a large square space. Curtains covered two full-length windows, and the big four-poster bed dominated one wall. Chests of drawers and chairs were placed around the room, and a long cheval mirror stood in one corner. "I can see why you always look so perfectly turned out if you spend your time gazing at yourself in that mirror."

Samuel laughed, some of the tension in his shoulders easing. "I am afraid to look at myself."

"I would not," Patricia cautioned, with raised eyebrows.

"Minx, you know I cannot resist a challenge. Oh, good lord! Look at the state of me!" Samuel groaned with real feelings of disgust. His shirt clung to him, filthy despite him being in the water for so long. His breeches would need to be burned by the look of them, his hair could only be described as wild, and his unshaven face looked back at him with some shame. "I cannot believe you married me, looking like this."

"I think the clergyman was concerned about the beast who stood before him," Patricia teased. She was nervous, worried and tired but tried to maintain a lightness, dampening down the feelings threatening to overwhelm her.

Samuel laughed but became serious when there was a tap on the door. Putting Patricia behind him, he shouted. "Who is it?"

"Bryant, m'lud."

"Come in."

The butler entered, carrying a large tray which contained a jug, glasses, and plates filled with thick sliced bread, chunks of ham and slices of cheese. There were also two generous pieces of apple pie with a jug of cream.

"Bryant, you are a saint," Samuel said. "This could very well be the best meal I have ever tasted."

As the butler placed the tray on one of the chests of drawers, his mouth twitched as he glanced over his shoulder for the briefest of moments. "I would not let Cook hear you say that, m'lud. You know what pride she takes in her work."

"After the last few days I have had, excepting the marriage to my wife, I can honestly say that this is the best thing I have had in a long time."

"In that case, I shall leave you be. Your pistols, as requested." Taking the four guns carefully out of his pockets, he handed them to Samuel, along with shot and powder. "I will remain on duty tonight."

"Thank you. I truly appreciate it," Samuel said.

"If there is a threat to this house, we all have a duty to be on the alert." Bryant left the room and closed the door behind him.

"It worries me a little that he is taking all of this completely in stride," Patricia said.

"That is what comes of being the butler to my mother for the last thirty years," Samuel said grimly. "I have never seen him other than perfectly in control, no matter how she behaved."

After eating their fill, Samuel loaded the pistols and handed the smaller two to Patricia. "I hate the fact that you might need these, but be assured that when we reach Bentham House, I will employ as many guards as are needed for you to feel safe."

"Stop worrying. I am sure they will soon catch up with the Barbosas. They will be desperate, after all," Patricia said.

"Desperate people do make mistakes, but they can also throw caution to the wind. The Barbosas, in particular, have nothing to lose."

"In that case, we need to be fully prepared. I am going to put one of the pistols in my pocket and the other near the fireplace," Patricia said.

"And I am going to try and make myself slightly more presentable. Then we can have a talk about this morning."

"It seems a long time ago," Patricia said, feeling desperately tired.

"Not long enough for the shock to ease at your words," Samuel said. Pulling out a clean shirt and breeches, he quickly changed, screwing the discarded clothing up and throwing it in a corner. Trying to get his hair in some sort of order, he rubbed his hand over his face. "I dare not risk trying to shave myself, I am likely to cut my throat. I am afraid this is the best I can do until I can beg the forgiveness of my valet for losing my boots and frock coat."

"He will be too busy being thankful for your safe return," Patricia said.

Samuel sat on the edge of the bed. "I have missed you today," he said, once more vulnerable. "I went from being the happiest of men to not knowing what had gone wrong."

"I have missed being close to you, too," Patricia acknowledged. "I just could not face a future in which you were intimate with others."

"But I will nev—What the devil is it now?" he ground out when a knock sounded at the door.

"Samuel, let me in. I need to speak to you," his mother said, twisting the knob which was locked.

"Mother, we will speak in the morning," Samuel answered through gritted teeth.

"If you do not open the door now, your mother will not live until morning. We have unfinished business, you and I. Let us in." Juliet's voice came through clearly.

"How the devil did she get in?" Samuel growled, striding to the door. "Go into the dressing room," he whispered to Patricia. "And stay there no matter what happens. I need to know you will be safe."

Chapter Twenty-One

S AMUEL COULD HAVE cursed Patricia when he noticed that the door leading into the dressing room had been left ajar. She was putting herself at risk when she should be keeping herself out of danger.

He opened the door, and was roughly pushed aside by Captain Barbosa.

"How did you get by my servants?" Samuel demanded, pushing himself off the chest of drawers he had been shoved into.

"They have some loyalty to your mother," Juliet said, a knife at his mother's throat.

"Let her go. Your argument is with me, not her."

"Oh, if it was only so simple," Juliet said. "She is going to be our ticket to gaining our freedom. And if you are wise, you will give us what we want without argument, for I have run out of patience with you."

"English pigs are all the same," Captain Barbosa spat.

"Delightful fellow, your father," Samuel said. "So, what do you need? Money? How will that help you? And why on earth did you come back to these shores, knowing that you will both hang if you're caught?"

"Our wealth is safely on board another ship. All we had on our persons was the necklace from you," Juliet snarled at him.

Samuel was playing for time. He hoped his servants were off to get help from Bow Street. All he could do was try and delay what would inevitably be the death of his mother and himself if he gave them what they wanted. "Ah, you did not appreciate my taste then?"

"Does your betrothed know that you gave her paste instead of real rubies and diamonds?" Juliet mocked. "Does she have any idea how little she means to you?"

"Oh, she means the world to me," Samuel said. "I can assure you that the necklace she wore was every bit the real thing. The one in the jewellery box... Well, you clearly found out how much that one was worth."

"I will enjoy killing you for that after you have watched your mother die," Juliet said.

"If you are expecting money and trinkets from me, you had better let my mother go."

"We are the ones giving the orders."

"Seems to me that it is just you giving the orders. Why do you not let your father speak?"

His words led to a babble of Spanish being uttered by Juliet, and Captain Barbosa grabbed Samuel and threw him with extreme force.

Sliding down the wall, Samuel had to admit that the course of action he had taken was not the best. Unfortunately, his pistols were on the chest of drawers next to the tray and completely out of his reach. He just had to keep going the way he was headed. Grimacing, he knew it was going to hurt.

"You are Spanish. I wondered why you accepted my mistakes when you were speaking Portuguese," he said conversationally, still sitting on the floor. "I take it you are sympathetic to Napoleon?"

"Why would you think that?"

Samuel laughed. "It was foolish of me, but I presumed you were sending money abroad or delivering it when you made your extra visits to ports. I should have guessed there was nothing but selfishness in your actions."

Juliet pressed the knife into his mother's neck, and she let out of squeal of pain. "You are wasting time. We should kill you both and then find our own money."

"We are the only ones who know where the money is kept."

"Then we only need one of you," Juliet said triumphantly. "Say goodbye to your mother."

PATRICIA HAD LEFT the door ajar purposely. She could not just walk away from Samuel, though that was what she thought she wanted when the doubts had crept in. Not wishing to share him with his mistresses was one thing, but she loved him more than anyone else in the world, and that was saying something when she was so close to Dominic and Enid.

She had taken the pistol out of her pocket as soon as the chamber door had opened. Peeping through the crack in the door, she had watched the scene unfold, her hand shaking so much, she had to hold it still with her other hand.

When Samuel had been thrown against the wall, she had almost let out a cry of despair; his body had been through so much in these last days. Knowing that he was trying to delay matters did not help the pain she felt when he remained on the floor, his face screwed up in agony.

Swallowing hard to try and steady her nerves, she was fully aware that time was running out for them. Juliet looked manic, and when she pressed the knife against Samuel's mother's neck, Patricia was sickened to see gleeful enjoyment in Juliet's smile. The woman was mad, and Patricia had to act.

When Juliet declared they only needed one of them alive to get what they wanted, Patricia didn't have much time to think. Juliet had only just uttered her final words before Patricia moved around the doorway, pointed her pistol and fired.

The expression on Juliet's face was that of shocked surprise as she released Samuel's mother, and her body was flung backwards as the bullet hit. The roar of anger that Captain Barbosa let out would have terrified anyone who heard it; it was so primal and fierce. He charged at Samuel, grabbing him off the floor in one swift move and shaking him as if he were nothing but a ragdoll.

Samuel's mother had fallen to the floor, but in a surprisingly agile move, she jumped up, grabbed the poker from the fireplace and started beating Captain Barbosa over the head.

As the captain crumpled to the floor, the room seemed to explode with men. They immediately grabbed Barbosa, dragging him away from Samuel.

Looking at his mother with an astonished smile, Samuel stood up. "I am impressed, Mother. I never dreamed you had it in you, but thank you. You could well have saved my life."

"You are the only thing I have done right in the world. That man was not going to hurt you while I had breath in my body."

Samuel looked dumbfounded at her words, then he noticed Patricia, rooted to the spot from where she had fired the pistol, staring at the prone body of Juliet. He crossed to her.

"I have killed her," she whispered as he enfolded her in his arms.

"You saved my mother's life and, because of that, my own," he said gently.

"But I have killed someone."

"She was about to commit murder, probably not for the first time. You did the right thing."

"It does not feel like it."

When Juliet's body was finally removed, and the Bow Street Officers had got statements from everyone, Samuel nodded to his mother. "We have a lot to talk about, but for now, can Patricia rest?"

"Of course. I take from the ring on her finger that she is now your wife?"

"Yes."

"I see. I will arrange for my things to be removed from my—her chamber."

"There is no need to hurry. She will be sharing my bed." Patricia had stiffened in Samuel's arms at his words, but had not tried to pull away.

His mother nodded at him. "Are you to remain in town?"

"No, we were going to go to Bentham House in the morning, and I would like to stick to that plan."

"I will remain here."

"I thought you might. But we shall have the dower house prepared for when you are ready to join us."

Without uttering another word, she left the room. "I think you have upset her," Patricia said.

"She will be fine. I have been surprised by her this evening. I never expected her to respond so effectively."

"She clearly cares for you a great deal in her own way."

"And do you care for me?" Patricia tried to pull away, but Samuel held onto her. "Please let me hold you," he said. "I have been struggling with the feeling that I am losing you all day, and I can hardly bear it. I was honestly considering offering myself as a willing sacrifice to Juliet."

"How can you say that?" Patricia looked at him for the first time—the anguish he was feeling was obvious.

"Because if you are not by my side, there is nothing for me to live for," he said. "I know that makes me sound like a tortured soul, but believe me when I say that being without you in my life is a thought I cannot stand. After experiencing the best night of my entire life, it has been followed by the worst of days. I would rather be thrown overboard and have cannon fire raging above my head than go through another day of not knowing whether or not I was going to lose you."

"It is just what you said about being unable to be a real husband. I know part of it was you teasing me, but I know you well enough to tell that there was meaning underneath the bluster."

"There was. But at that point, I had not seen what was before me. I had mistakenly presumed that we would be friends forever, and I thought that was enough for me, for no one could compare to you. From almost the first moment of us pretending to be engaged, it was as if my eyes had finally opened. I was in love with you and had been for goodness knows how long."

"I felt the same."

"Then why are you doubting my feelings now?"

"Because it is common knowledge that you tire of your mistresses. How will your wife be different?"

"Sometimes I really wish we were not such good friends, for you have far too much information that you can use against me. I am going to admit this once, and once only. If you mention any of it to Dominic, I will deny it utterly."

"I would never tell Dominic anything private between us."

"You spoiled me for anyone else. I did not stick with any of the others because they were not *you*. I might not have acknowledged that I was in love with you, but deep down, I knew. Whenever I saw a tall woman with hair similar to yours, I would try to like her, but I never could. Then I would try with a woman whose intelligence compared with yours, but she would look nothing like you. I was going through life trying to find you when *you* were there all the time. I will never seek anyone else because I finally have you."

"You always say the right things, but—"

"No buts, Patricia. You are either with me for the rest of our days or not. I cannot do half measures, and if you are concerned about jealousy, I will try my best not to draw the cork of every man who looks at you with appreciation. Perhaps if I promise to only hit half of them, I might be able to achieve that."

Patricia laughed. "You are ridiculous."

"I am yours, and I hope you are mine."

"I am," Patricia finally acknowledged. "I think I always have been, but self-doubt last night made me question everything."

"In the future, when you wake up in the night with fears or doubts, I wish you to wake me. We will either talk it through, or I will prove to you with actions that your thoughts are unfounded."

"Thank you for indulging me. I never considered myself a wet goose, but I am shocked at my sudden fears. After all, I know you are such a good man. But I could not help myself." She shook her head. "I am sorry. I would hate to turn into the type of feeble woman that I have always disliked."

"For me, you are perfect. You have beguiled me like no one else ever could."

"Beguiled?"

"It is not nice to laugh at your husband; his self-worth could be hurt. You know what a gentle soul I am."

She was unable to argue when he picked her up and took her to bed, showing her just how much fun teasing a besotted husband could turn out to be.

Epilogue

A S SAMUEL HAD predicted, there were no recriminations from Dominic towards Patricia. In fact, he had embraced her so hard on first hearing about what happened that Patricia had begged to be released from his hold.

Juliet's father was given a harsh sentence, as were many of the crew who had followed him willingly. The other members of the crew were dispersed throughout the company. Bates enjoyed a visit to the Scilly Isles, it being warmer than England but still close enough to home. He found that he was happy being ashore after all and, with Samuel's help, bought a cottage overlooking the busy harbour where he could watch the comings and goings and pass the time of day with other visiting sailors.

The Albers family moved to the Bentham estate. Mr. Albers always suffered with his back, so he stayed home while his wife worked with the local milliner. She had a real talent, and Patricia bought all her bonnets from her and promoted her whenever she was in town.

Admitting the deception to her friends was never going to be easy, but as Amelia had predicted, they understood and were delighted that Patricia had finally got her happy ever after.

Two years later, Patricia found herself inside a church, struggling with a fidgeting little boy. Finally, she gave in and handed him back to his nanny, who took him outside to run free while the ceremony took place. She smiled as Samuel took hold of her hand.

"I told you he would never sit still," he whispered to her.

"I know it was a vain hope, but I had to try."

"As long as it has not tired you out." Samuel rubbed the back of his hand gently across the soft swell of her stomach.

"I am fine. I just hope this is a quiet little girl."

Samuel managed to turn the laugh into a cough, but Dominic shot him a look over his shoulder. "You do know who her mother is, don't you?" he whispered before receiving a poke to his ribs with a carefully aimed elbow.

"I think it is time to join Dominic," Patricia said. "He needs you."

"Only for the formalities." Samuel winked. "We know he will be perfectly fine now he has finally chosen the right woman."

Moving out of the pew, Samuel quickly went to stand beside Dominic as the music started, and the congregation in the church rose to greet the bride.

Patricia handed Enid a handkerchief when she heard a sniff. "What do I need this for? I am not crying," Enid hissed at her.

"Of course you are not." Patricia smiled, turning to watch her future sister-in-law enter the church. "She looks beautiful."

"That is because I chose her and helped them along," Enid said, openly dabbing her eyes.

"Do not let Dominic hear you saying that. He thinks he fell in love without any help at all."

"Everyone needs a little push now and then."

"I cannot argue with that," Patricia said, smiling at Samuel. Her husband was not the only one beguiled. And she had never been happier.

The End

Author's Note

I have had the fortune to live a dream. I've always wanted to write, but life got in the way as it so often does until a few years ago. Then a change in circumstance enabled me to do what I loved: sit down to write. Now writing has taken over my life, holidays being based around research, so much so that no matter where we go, my long-suffering husband says, "And what connection to the Regency period has this building/town/garden got?"

That dream became a little more surreal when in 2018, I became an Amazon StorytellerUK Finalist with Lord Livesey's Bluestocking. A Regency Romance in the top five of an all-genre competition! It was a truly wonderful experience, I didn't expect to win, but I had a ball at the awards ceremony.

I do appreciate it when readers get in touch, especially if they love the characters as much as I do. Those first few weeks after release is a trying time; I desperately want everyone to love my characters that take months and months of work to bring to life.

If you enjoy the books please would you take the time to write a review on Amazon? Reviews are vital for an author, although I admit to bad ones being crushing. Selfishly I want readers to love my stories!

I can be contacted for any comments you may have, via my website:

www.audreyharrison.co.uk

or

facebook.com/AudreyHarrisonAuthor

Please sign-up for email/newsletter—only sent out when there is something to say!

www.audreyharrison.co.uk

You'll receive a free copy of The Unwilling Earl in mobi/epub format for signing-up as a thank you!

About the Author

Audrey lives in the North West of England (a Lancashire Lass) and is of the opinion that she was born about two hundred years too late, especially when dealing with technology! She is a best-selling author of Historical Romance, especially the Regency period.

In the real world she has always longed to write, writing a full manuscript when she was fourteen years old. Work, marriage and children got in the way as they do and it was only when an event at work landed her in hospital that she decided to take stock. One Voluntary Redundancy later, she found that the words and characters came to the forefront and the writing began in earnest.

So, although at home more these days, the housework is still neglected and meals are still late on the table, but she has an understanding family, who usually shake their heads at her and sigh. That is a sign of understanding, isn't it?

Find out more at:

www.audreyharrison.co.uk

or

facebook.com/AudreyHarrisonAuthor

or

Audrey Harrison (@audrey.harrisonauthor) • Instagram photos and videos

Printed in Great Britain
by Amazon

29805061R10129